THE LADY NEXT DOOR

S. E. GREEN

Copyright © S. E. Green, 2022

The right of S. E. Green to be identified as the author of this work has been asserted per the Copyright, Designs and Patents Act 1976. All rights reserved. No part of this publication may be reproduced, transmitted, or stored in a retrieval system, in any form or by any means, without permission in writing from the publisher, nor be otherwise circulated in any form of binding or cover other than that in which it is published and without a similar condition being imposed on the subsequent purchaser. All characters in this publication are fictitious and any resemblance to real people, alive or dead, is purely coincidental.

PROLOGUE

It's hard digging a grave.

1

Thursday 6:30 a.m.

LAUGHING, I race after Popeye, my two-year-old rescue beagle. He darts and swerves, following his nose and not my voice. He's got a hell of a pace when he wants to.

Across my lawn he goes, the next one as well, and over onto the new neighbor's. He heads straight up the porch and through her open door, following the scent of breakfast.

"Popeye!" I vault the front steps in one leap, coming to a stop in an airy foyer.

With flat-ironed, chin-length black hair, no makeup, and a lean build, a woman kneels next to Popeye. Rubbing under his chin, she smiles as she looks up at me. "I take it this cutie belongs to you?"

"Yes. I'm so sorry." I hold up the leash. "I know better than to take this off of him."

"That's okay. I love dogs." Wearing green striped pajama

bottoms and a pink tank top, she stands. "Can he have a bite of waffle?"

"Sure."

She motions me to follow her down the hall to the kitchen. Popeye leads the way, his nails clicking on the hardwood floors. Unopened boxes line the walls. Furniture, too, still in plastic.

"I'm Jessica," I say. "I live two houses over. Welcome to the street."

"Martha," she tells me, cutting off through an archway and into the kitchen. She walks over to the counter where a plate with waffles sits. She wedges off a tiny bit that Popeye eagerly swallows.

She offers me some, but I decline. "I already ate."

"Sucks for you," she jokes, eating the rest of what she gave my dog. "Because I make some killer blueberry waffles."

I like her. "Where ya from?"

"Florida."

"Me, too. What part?"

"South near Miami."

"North for me. The Jacksonville area."

"It's a long state."

"That it is."

Martha nods out the open kitchen window to her back yard where redbuds are in full bloom. Beyond that, a tall wood fence separates our homes from the neighborhood behind us. "I can't get over the colors here and the weather." She sighs, and that one exhalation has a dreamy note to it. "It's tranquil. My little oasis."

"Welcome to Virginia then. I've been here five years. No regrets." I look around the kitchen, noting the freshly painted eggshell-colored walls. "I saw workers over here. I figured the new owners were doing some touch-ups. The walls used to be papered with giant blue and silver flowers."

"I know. It was one of the things I negotiated when I bought the home. The paper had to go."

"Wise."

"So, you knew the prior owners?"

"Sort of. They were elderly. I came over a few times if they needed help with something."

"That's nice of you."

"So sad when he passed. I was here for the wake." Leaning down, I clip the leash on Popeye. "Well, anyway, I have to get to work, and you have a house to unpack."

"I take it from your cartoon print scrubs that you work in medicine?"

"I do. I'm a nurse at the hospital. Pediatric ward. How about you?"

She laughs. "You're not going to believe this, but I'm also a nurse."

"Get out. Where do you work?"

"Home health care. I took some time off, though. I don't start for another two weeks."

I wave my arm around her kitchen. "I love organizing. If you need help unpacking, let me know."

"Heck, I'll take you up on that. Want to come over later?"

"Oh…" I chuckle, not expecting such a quick invite. "Um, sure. I work a twelve-hour shift, though, so it'll be after seven."

"All good."

"Okay. I'll bring wine. You like Chinese?"

"I sure do."

"I know a great place. We'll get delivery."

"Sounds fun. It'll be my treat." She walks me out.

2

Thursday 7:30 p.m.

Though I'm only hanging out with a new friend, I still double-check myself in the mirror. I run a wide-tooth comb through my long, wavy brown hair, swipe tinted Chapstick across my lips, and dab on a bit of foundation.

I use to wear my hair just like Martha's. Maybe I'll cut mine again. I did like it short.

With Popeye fed, I rub his ears goodbye. Then with a wine bottle in hand, I walk the short distance to Martha's place. It's not quite dark yet, but it will be soon, signaled by the exterior home lights flicking on up and down our small street of Cape Cod homes.

This time her front door is closed. I note a security camera in the upper right corner. That wasn't there earlier. Assuming it is on, I wave before ringing her bell.

It takes her a lot longer than expected to answer, and breathing heavy, she steps aside. "Come in."

"Where did you come from?"

"The basement."

"We don't have those in Florida." I step inside. "They're pretty handy."

"What have you done with yours?"

"Storage. You?"

"A secure bunker for when the Zombie Apocalypse happens."

I'm not sure if she's kidding. But then she grins slyly and I roll my eyes. Like me, she's dressed casually in leggings and an oversized tee. She closes the front door. It thuds so authoritatively that I jump.

"I've got to get that fixed. It's like a haunted house." She lowers her voice to a dramatic spooky pitch. "You can come in, but you're not leaving."

Immediately to the left, a stairwell goes up to the second floor. Like earlier, she leads the way down the hall toward the kitchen. On the left, we pass a living room and on the right an eating area—both with open archways.

"There used to be doors here." My fingers trail over the woodwork. "I like that you took them out. Really opens things up."

We step into the kitchen. She already has two stemmed glasses out with a wine opener beside them.

"There were boxes everywhere earlier." I look around. "You got a lot done today."

"The thought of a friend coming over motivated me."

It's silly, but I love that she just referred to me as her friend.

While she uncorks the malbec I brought, I put my keys and phone down and recite the Chinese menu by heart. She interrupts me saying, "Tofu lo mein with a spring roll. Also, I can't believe you know their menu like that."

"I should. I order nearly every week. Tofu? Are you a vegetarian?"

"Vegan."

"Me, too."

She holds the wine bottle up. "By the way, malbec is my favorite."

"Mine as well." As I dial the number for food, I say, "Florida, nursing, eating habits, wine…seems we have a lot in common."

Smiling, she pours our wine while I order. After I hang up, she hands me my glass and we clink.

"To new friends," she says, and we sip. "Tour?"

"Sure."

"This is the kitchen. Obviously." To the right yet another archway leads back into the eating area. There used to be a wall there. Now the downstairs has a good flow. She points to a closed door in the corner. "Through there is the basement. I won't bore you with that." She motions to the bank of windows and door that overlooks her backyard. "I'm probably going to do some sort of French doors there."

I nod.

Carrying her wine, she walks from the kitchen. Before we reach the living room, she pauses to open a narrow door, showing me a downstairs half bath. She closes it. Her excitement is evident when she says, "Now, let me show what I did upstairs."

I follow her back down the hall, noting she kept the espresso-stained hard wood floors intact. At the front door, we turn right, and I'm behind her as we tread up the narrow steps that creak on our ascent.

Halfway up she pauses to jump on a particularly

squeaky one. "I could've got that fixed but I like the creak. It makes the house seem old."

"It *is* old."

She laughs.

At the top, she stops. With giddy eyes, she looks back at me. "The times you were over here, did you ever come upstairs?"

"No."

"It used to be three bedrooms and two baths. You ready for this?" She takes the last step and I'm right behind her as we move into one giant open room.

I suck in a breath. "Oh my God! It's like my Pinterest board come to life."

She knocked down all the walls to make an airy and open master suite complete with a bay window, a reading corner, a canopy bed that sits high off the floor, a home office, a modular closet, a Pilates reformer, and a spa-inspired bathroom—all done in deep mauve and powder blue.

I am in total awe as I slowly walk around. "I'm serious. I'll have to show you my Pinterest account. This is my dream. You missed your calling. You should have been an interior designer."

"Definitely my hobby."

"What about guests?"

"What about them? This is my home. I make it for me, not them. They can stay at a hotel." She toasts the air, then sips.

"Martha, I do like you."

"Come on." She leads the way back downstairs.

In the living room, we make ourselves comfortable on a light gray sectional couch with dark gray accent pillows. A matching rectangular ottoman takes up the area where a coffee table typically goes. On top sits a sturdy stone and wood tray that she places her wine glass on. I do the same. Large square windows give a view of the side yard where a row of towering magnolias offers privacy from the house next door.

"When did you move in?" I ask.

"Officially, yesterday. I've been living in a hotel while the renovations were getting done." She waves an arm around. "So, tell me about yourself and this neighborhood I've moved to. I need all the gossip."

"Well, let's see. I'm thirty-five and that makes me the youngest person on the street. That is unless you're younger?"

"Thirty-six."

"Ah, then my record reigns. I'm divorced. No kids. Single. Moved here for a fresh start. I work a lot. You know I'm a nurse. I love-love-love hiking. That's typically what I do on days off. There are a lot of trails around here if you ever want to join me on one of my outings."

"I'll totally do that."

"Cool." I point toward the windows where the magnolias grow. "There's an Airbnb right beside you. The owners are super picky about who they rent to. So, don't worry about noise or anything. On the other side of them is me. You'll have to come over and lend your decorating hand."

"Deal."

I nod toward the other side of the house beyond the dining room. "Right beside you in that direction is an elderly deaf man. He just turned eighty-six. On the other side of him is an older couple who recently retired, bought one of those big RVs, and took off. That's it. That's our street. Five houses total. It's very quiet. And the best part—all those woods our homes face? It's protected land. No one will ever build."

"Exactly what I want."

Picking up my glass, I take a sip. "Your turn."

Amusement tickles her features. "I think we're each other's doppelgänger. I'm also divorced. No kids. Came here for a fresh start. And while I'm not as avid of a hiker as you seem to be, I do love a good trail."

"Martha, I think we were meant to meet."

"Jessica, I do believe you are correct."

We toast again.

The bell rings with our Chinese food.

"That was quick." Martha gets up. "Like I said, my treat."

"Then I'll get next time."

"One of many meals to come."

3

Thursday 10:30 p.m.

With the bottle I brought over gone, one of hers gone, and Chinese food eaten, we've moved on to drinking a third bottle and raiding her kitchen.

"It has been so long since I hung out with a girlfriend," Martha says, her mouth full of wheat crackers. "We're going to be so hungover tomorrow."

"Yep. Good thing I'm off for the next three days." I down a handful of granola clusters. "Yum. What brand is this?"

"I made it."

"Ah, and there is where our differences are. I'm an expert at ordering Uber Eats."

"Cooking is my jam. I'll totally teach you."

I crinkly my nose. "No, thanks."

She snorts and we both think that's the funniest sound ever. Laughing, we stagger from the kitchen back down the hall into the living room, carrying freshly poured wine. Together we slide onto the couch. I put entirely too much effort into placing my glass on the ottoman's wood and stone tray.

Outside, the night has set in with no stars, only clouds predicting rain. It'll be a good day tomorrow to nurse a hangover.

One lone unpacked box sits beside the entertainment center. Bleary-eyed, Martha eyes it. Her words come slurred. "I could've unpacked that. I saved it for us. You *were* coming over to help me after all. There's one in the kitchen also."

"We'll unpack them. I promise."

She drinks half of her wine. "You're a bad influence. I can't remember the last time I drank this much."

"I *am* a bad influence. You are correct."

Another snort as she puts her glass next to mine. "We look about the same size. We should share closets."

"I love that idea, especially if you shop at Athleta."

"Will Prana work?"

"Oh, yeah."

Martha stretches back on the sectional, propping her feet on the ottoman. I do the same, thinking we should probably drink some water.

"You got family around here?" she asks.

"No. My dad still lives in Florida. We're not that close. We speak on holidays and birthdays. I've got a mom somewhere. Haven't talked to her since I was a teenager."

"What happened?"

"She decided she didn't like being a mom, I guess."

"I'm sorry."

"Thanks."

"Siblings?"

"Nope. You?"

"Kind of the same situation. I'm an only child. My parents died when I was seventeen."

"Oh, wow."

"It's okay. Long time ago."

The mood in the room dips. I try to think of something funny to say, but I come up blank.

"Why divorced?" she asks.

Shaking my head, I close my eyes. This is not a topic I want to get into right now. "Summary: he was controlling. It's a long story. Another day."

Martha yawns. "Another day."

Silence fills the room as we both drift in our alcohol buzz. Though my eyes are closed, the room still spins.

Most of my friends at the hospital are married with kids. It's few and far I do things with them. This will be great, having Martha nearby. "I've always wanted to hike the Grand Canyon. Maybe I can talk you into that. I want to do the rim-to-rim one where you stay overnight at the bottom." One of my eyes opens back up. I survey her stretched out in the other corner. I think she passed out.

She murmurs, "If there's a hot tub and martini at the bottom I'm in."

The laugh that comes from me is so quick and unexpected that spit sprays.

"I'm going to go to sleep now." A loopy grin curls her lips. "Night-night."

"Night-night." I slide from the sectional sofa onto the cool hardwood floor. "I like it down here better." I sprawl out, my arms and legs wide. I should get up and go home, but I can't move. The alcohol tugs me further down, and as I sink into the blurry pull of drunk exhaustion, I think of Popeye.

He'll be fine until the morning...

4

T *hursday 11:51 p.m.*

A HARD BOOZY sleep takes hold. I dream of drifting through clouds and gliding down rainbows. I become a snake, slinking through canyons. I grow legs and run through a city. That city turns into a small town. Now I'm back here in my neighborhood, standing outside of this house, looking around. I'm wearing a ski mask because I'm an intruder. I try the front door. It doesn't open. I tread the porch. At the living room window, I peer in, seeing two women—one on the sofa and one on the floor. I try to open the window, but it's locked. I step off the porch. In the side yard, I look up to the second story, spying a cracked window. Perfect. Now, I just need a ladder...

With a soft groan, I press my fingers into my eye sockets. What a weird dream. Alcohol sucks. I knew better. I am going to suffer so badly in the morning. Groggily, I sit up. I look around for water, seeing only our wine glasses still balanced on the ottoman's tray.

Martha lies face down, one arm dragging the floor and a leg shoved under a cushion.

My head is killing me. I need to chug water, but I lie back down instead. I'm just about to pass out again when a sudden uneasiness creeps along my skin. My eyes open. I stare at the smooth white ceiling of the living room, my ears tuned. But I hear nothing other than the pattering of light rain.

I sit up again, looking over to the windows where a few drops trail the dark glass. There are no wonky shadows or weird lights. Still, I stay very quiet, listening, eyeing the dimness. Gradually my bleary alcohol head creeps back in. I climb to my knees. On a dizzy wave, I squeeze my eyes shut. My hands come out, steading my equilibrium on the ottoman. When I feel ready, I stand up and shifting around the sectional couch, I make my way through the archway into the hall.

The walls drift past as I shuffle toward the kitchen.

At the refrigerator, I open the door. Harsh light drills into my skull. Squinting, I eye several water bottles. My fingers fumble for one and with it in hand, I gratefully close the door.

As I drink, I search through the kitchen drawers, looking for Advil. I find Tylenol instead and take three.

Overhead a floorboard creaks. I pause, looking up. Water rushes through the pipes and it startles me. This is an old home. Mine does the same. Yet I stare at the ceiling. I swear I hear feet. In the living room, the sofa squeaks. Martha heaves a heavy sigh.

For a moment, I hold steady. Silence grows.

Wonky imagination, I tell myself as I trek back into the

living room. Martha's now face up. I look at the floor where I just spent the last several hours. It no longer looks inviting. I should probably just go home.

I walk over to the window that looks out over the side yard and magnolia trees. I freeze. A ladder's been propped against the side of the house. That wasn't there before.

"M-Martha," I whisper.

Overhead, another floorboard creaks.

I move, leaping across the living room and dropping down next to her. Grabbing her shoulders, I shake her. "Wake up. Wake up."

But she's in a profound drunken sleep.

Overhead, another creak—this one closer to the stairs.

Desperately, I shake her. "Wake up. Come on. Come on."

There's a little water left in my bottle. I unscrew the lid and pour it over her head.

Now she's awake. And pissed. She sits straight up, sputtering, and shouts, "WHAT THE HELL?"

Slamming my hand over her mouth, I drag her off the couch. "Someone's here," I whisper. "In the house."

Heavy footsteps move, fast. Whoever is up there heard her.

We race out of the living room. I yank her toward the front door right as the footsteps pound down the stairs. The intruder's shadow precedes him, tall and threatening, with a gun held outstretched in his hand.

We jerk to a halt.

We're blocked. We'll never get the door unlocked and both of us out in time.

Martha clutches me. *The back door*, she mouths. I nod.

Silently, we duck into the eating area, cut through to the kitchen, and race over to the back door. But it's locked. I jiggle the knob, noting we need a key.

Shaking her head, Martha yanks me over to the basement door. I didn't see it before, but a keypad has been mounted beside it. Frantically, she punches in numbers. The intruder moves down the hallway. His footsteps pause in the archway of the living room.

The basement door opens. She skitters inside. The intruder makes it to the kitchen. Through a ski mask that he wears, his eyes meet mine. He lunges right as Martha yanks me into the basement and slams the door.

We trip over each other, nearly tumbling down the steps. My arms come out for balance but they meet air. There is no railing or walls. I almost fall over the side.

She's a few steps below me. "Get the light," she says. "Switch is at the top."

I move back up. My hands slide up and down the brick wall. I feel another keypad before finding the switch. I flick it on. It casts the basement in a dim white glow.

For several seconds, we don't move. Our heavy breaths fill the air. We stare at each other, scared out of our minds.

Gradually, her pale face gains color.

Gradually, my racing heart slows.

Together we descend the wood steps, coming down to the concrete basement floor. Shelves line the wall to the left, filled with supplies—water, food, first aid, tools, and various other things. A foldable desk holds an extra-large monitor with a small laptop attached and a padded metal chair underneath. In the corner is an oversized beanbag.

I turn a slow circle, confused. With brick walls and a concrete floor, this room is about twelve-by-twelve which is only half the size of my basement. Also, "Where's the door out?"

"Don't have one."

"What do you mean you don't have one? Why the hell did we come down here? I thought you had a door out?"

"I'm sorry. I knew we'd be safe. That's all I was thinking of."

Jesus Christ.

She looks like she's about to cry.

With a sigh, I turn away, looking back up the steps. This side of the door is steel. She wasn't kidding about a Zombie Apocalypse bunker.

She says, "My father was an Army Ranger. He always said to prepare for the worst. This is my 'worst' room. I never imagined I'd be using it."

"My father's a retired Marine. I get it." With another sigh, I turn back to see her sitting on the padded chair and looking at the giant external monitor. It shows a split screen with several interior and exterior views of the house including the porch, the back yard, the hallway, the door down here to the basement, the upstairs master suite, the side yard, and various others.

What the hell?

I move in, looking over her shoulder. An average-sized man, dressed in black cargo pants, a long black athletic shirt, and a ski mask, throws all his weight into the basement door. He kicks it. He punches it. Chest heaving, he stares at it before trying again. From this side, I hear none of his rage.

"Reinforced steel," Martha says.

"Please tell me there's a phone down here or that computer has an internet connection."

"No. Not yet at least. I only just today set up the cameras. I was going to finish connecting the alarm system this week."

"Where are all those cameras?"

"Most are hidden. You're not meant to see them."

I barely have time to digest how odd that is. "I can't believe this is happening. There has never been a break-in on this street."

Nibbling the inside of her cheek, Martha stares at the large screen. "We're just going to have to wait him out, I guess."

I move in closer, watching the man pace the kitchen. I note a "Talk" button on the screen. "Click that. Tell him to take what he wants and leave."

"I'm not sure if it even works."

"Well click it and see."

She does, leaning forward to speak, "Take what you want and leave."

In the kitchen, the man whips around, searching where the voice came from. From the angle, it looks like she mounted the camera above the refrigerator.

"Apparently, he can hear you." Taking the mouse from her, I click the "Talk" button. "What do you want?"

His gaze narrows in on a spot above the refrigerator. He found the camera. He holds up a gloved finger, wagging it back and forth like he's saying, naughty-naughty girls.

"Can we hear him?" I ask.

"I think so. I don't know. Like I said, I just put this in. I haven't played around with it yet." She leans in. "What is he doing?"

We watch as he rifles through her kitchen drawers. He finds a notepad and marker, writes something, and holds it up to the camera.

I'M HERE FOR YOU

5

Thursday 11:59 p.m.

MARTHA GASPS.

My heart kicks in. I take a breath. "Wh-who is that?"

"This is not happening." She grabs her head.

"What's not happening?"

"I think I'm going to be sick." She turns away from the desk and drops her head between her knees. "No-no-no, this is not happening. I don't know how he found me."

"Who?"

"I was so careful."

"WHO?"

She lifts her head, peering at me through bloodshot, helpless eyes. "My ex-husband."

For several long seconds, we stare at each other. I'm the first to turn away, pacing a small circle. My thoughts tumble and spin. I think of my own ex-husband and the tumultuous relationship that I ran from. And...I get it.

"Martha, our parallel lives are freaking me out."

"What are you talking about?" she mumbles.

"Everything including the fact I also ran from an ex-husband." I stop pacing to look at her.

"Did you change your name?" she asks.

"No. Are you telling me it was so bad you had to change *your* name?"

"Yes, my last name. He's a horrible man. Said he'd hunt me down and kill me. That wasn't just a threat." She stands up, pointing at the screen. "You see that gun? He will use it. I promise you that." She waves her arms around the basement. "My ex is the real reason why I have this 'worst' room. I just never thought he'd find me." Tears fill her eyes. "I'm so naïve. And now I've pulled you into this."

Crossing the small distance, I grab her shoulders and look her in the eyes. "We're going to figure this out. I promise."

6

Friday 1 a.m.

WE'VE BEEN in the basement for an hour watching her ex-husband walk around the first floor, closing all the blinds and surveying the rooms. He's yet to take his ski mask off and I can only assume it's because of the cameras.

Quinn, my ex, was a paranoid, controlling man who lost his temper nearly every day. He never once hit me, but he used words. So many horrible words. In one of my rare conversations with my father, he said to me, *Jessica, if you can see yourself in ten years and you're happy, then stay. If not, then go. Life is short.*

Dad was so right.

But the night before I left was the worst night ever. I saw a side of Quinn that only cemented my decision. I left the next morning. Unfortunately, he wouldn't respect my choice. Intimidating phone calls, threatening texts, and eventually stalking led me to file a restraining order. It was only after I changed my phone number and email and moved states away, that I never heard from him again.

That's been five years ago now.

Martha stands in front of the shelves—three total, each stretching the length of the left wall with the top one tall enough to require the step stool propped against the wall. Quietly, she surveys the items. From the second shelf, she brings down a large first aid kit and rifles through it, locating headache pills. On the bottom shelf is an open milk crate filled with Larabars, organic juice boxes, snack bags of dried fruits and nuts, and various other things that I have in my panty as well. After taking the headache pills and drinking all of one apple juice box she offers me some, but I decline. I'm plenty sober now.

"Well, at least we won't starve," she tries to make a joke.

I sit down at the desk and click the mouse around the small laptop. There's nothing on this thing but the security app. "You must have some way to reach the outside."

"I don't." Closing the first aid kit, she slides it back onto the second shelf.

"How is that even possible?" I hover the mouse over the Wi-Fi connection but no networks come up, not even a home network. "How are the cameras connected?"

"Hard wired. I bought one of those systems with both, but the installation guy only did the wiring. We were supposed to schedule a follow-up for him to finish. If my ex would've broken in this time next week the whole place would've lit up. There would be triggers on the windows and a way for me to dial out from down here."

I know next to nothing about security systems. Yet I click around a little more. "Is this recording?"

"Live feed only."

On the screen, her ex opens and closes kitchen cabinets and drawers.

Martha plops down in the beanbag. "I was so careful about selecting this neighborhood. This house. I changed my last name. I did what I could in cash. I even cut and colored my hair. I met you and thought, 'Hey, my first friend in forever.' I swear to God, I can't win."

"You cut and colored your hair?"

"I'm a dirty blonde."

"Funny enough, my hair used to look like yours—color and cut both."

With an unamused chuckle, she shakes her head. "We are each other's twin."

We share a tired smile that dies away.

"What are we going to do?" I ask.

"It'll be days before anyone comes looking for you, right? Didn't you say you have the next three days off?"

I nod.

"And I don't start my new job for two weeks." Her eyes widen. "Oh my God, Popeye."

Shit. "I think he'll be okay. I have a doggie door to my backyard. I also have one of those endless water machines and a food toy where he can retrieve cookies, with effort. Point is, he won't starve. He'll hate me, but he'll be okay."

"Still..."

My poor dog's going to be traumatized.

Pushing up out of the padded chair, I walk over to the shelves. A toolbox sits on top with a camping stove beside it and an unattached propane tank. A box next to it is labeled OLD STUFF. Another box is labeled TOYS. On the second shelf, there are folded blankets and a box labeled CLOTHES. The bottom shelf has mostly food, plus adult diapers. Maybe the elderly couple who lived here before Martha left those.

"Do you think he'll eventually leave?" I turn from the shelves to see her staring over at a ceiling vent. It's oversized and rectangular-shaped, positioned in the corner on the other side of the steps.

"We're both pretty skinny but if you're thinking of shimmying out via that vent, it's not going to work," I say.

Martha tries to push a smile across her face, but it dashes just as quickly as it appeared.

"Where does that go?" I ask.

"The kitchen, I think."

"Do you think he can hear us talking?"

She shrugs.

Together, we look back at the monitor.

Her ex found our phones and is currently waving them back and forth in front of the camera, making sure we see he's about to toss them into a sink full of water. He does, and they quickly sink. Not satisfied, he retrieves them, putting them on a butcher block. Using a meat mallet that he took from a drawer, he pounds each phone into a crumbled mess.

"He could've just taken the SIM cards out," I mumble.

"He's not very bright."

We share a chuckle.

Back on the monitor, he places an orange case on the counter and opens it. It's a drill.

"Where did he get that?" I ask.

"From under the kitchen sink."

Pausing, he studies the basement door. He picks up the meat mallet and a butter knife, looking between them. What is he doing? He moves across the kitchen to the basement. He begins using the mallet as a hammer and the knife as a screwdriver to remove the large pins holding the door's hinges.

For someone "not very bright" that's pretty smart.

But Martha said it's reinforced steel. I look up the steps to this side of the door. Like before, I hear nothing of what he's doing on the other side. "He can't get through this side, right? That's what you said."

Martha doesn't answer me.

I look over at her, noting she's now lying back in the beanbag with her eyes closed.

"Are you okay?"

Her hands tremble as she brings them up to cover her ears.

"Martha?"

Though she's reclined back, she rocks in the beanbag.

I cross over, kneeling beside her. "Listen, you can't do this. You're about to have a panic attack. You have to focus."

"He's going to get in," she whimpers.

Firmly, I grasp her calf. "No, he won't get through this side. You said it's reinforced steel. That means we're safe. *You're* safe."

Martha shakes her head.

It alarms me. "Why are you shaking your head? Please tell me it's reinforced steel. You cannot do this. You're freaking me out."

Her breath catches. Oh, crap. She's about to nose dive into a full-on panic attack.

My first inclination is to slap it out of her, but I make myself calm down. Two of us in hysterics will do no good.

She seems to lose her balance as her body sinks further into the beanbag.

Launching into a nursing mode, I press my fingers to her

wrist. Her pulse is a bit fast, but not bad. "Have you ever had a panic attack before?"

Her head jerks with a "no."

I had one back in college. Oddly enough, it was Quinn who got me through it. "Think of something spacious and lovely," I say. "Where's your favorite place?"

"P-parks."

"Okay, you're in the middle of a park. You're alone on a large lawn, lying on the grass. It's spring and the sun sparkles overhead. You stretch your arms and legs out, soaking in the warmth. You're happy, out in the open. All around you, flowers grow. You might pick some later. It's beautiful, this park, and so wide open. You breathe slowly, taking it in. Breathe with me now, Martha, in, out, in. Slowly."

She does, inhaling fast through the nose and blowing out forcefully through the mouth. "It's like the walls are pushing in."

I nod. "Slower."

She repeats, inhaling fast through the nose, then out forcefully through the mouth. "It's like the room is warping."

I nod. "Slower."

She doesn't listen. In fast. Out forcefully.

In fast. Out forcefully.

In fast. Out forcefully.

Nothing about her is calming down. It's escalating.

I slap her.

Her eyes fly open. Her hands drop from her ears. Panic converts to anger. She shoves me. "Don't touch me!"

"Well, at least now you're coherent."

Glaring at me, she puts her hand over her cheek. I glare right back.

"Just give me a minute," she snaps, shoving up out of the beanbag.

She charges over to the screen where her ex is about to fully remove the second pin. "I don't suppose my elderly deaf neighbor will suddenly get his hearing back?" she asks, her voice no longer panicky and now angry.

I'm glad to hear the change. I prefer her fury. "Not likely."

"I don't suppose someone will rent the Airbnb next to me," she bites off.

"Probably not."

We watch as her ex takes the door away. The steel one greets him. It takes him a second to register what he's looking at, then he loses it again—kicking and punching and hammering at it with the meat mallet.

He takes the drill and puts it dead center. Sparks fly, but no hole emerges. One of those sparks pings his ski mask. Yelping, he jumps back.

I smirk.

As her ex stomps off, I carefully survey the dimensions of the kitchen floor, comparing it to the basement. I look again at the vent on the other side of the wood steps. "I don't think that vent goes to the kitchen. I think it goes into the living room. Where's the key to the back door?"

"I don't remember. Maybe one of the kitchen drawers? Or maybe it's on my key ring in my purse. I don't know."

"I might have an idea."

7

Friday 2 a.m.

Using the step stool, I bring down the small propane tank, the mid-sized green and white toolbox, a yellow and black flashlight, and a roll of duct tape. I select both Phillips-head and flat-head screwdrivers.

Martha helps me carry everything over to the vent. After positioning the step stool, I climb up. Balanced on my tiptoes, I work at removing the vent's cover. With only two screws holding it in place, it comes off easily. Beyond that sits a crossbar that I wedge out with the flat head screwdriver. It gives me access to the duct work.

Using the flashlight, I peer up into the darkness. "Looks like it curves to the right, which would put it into the living room." *Hopefully.*

"Are you sure about this?"

"No. But I saw it in a movie."

"This isn't a movie."

I look down at her. "I know that." I hand her everything I'm holding. "Duct tape please."

She holds the flashlight as I tear off several lengths of the silver tape and seal the vent, leaving enough room for my arm and the small propane tank.

Next comes the gas.

A knob and release valve are already attached to the tank. I rotate the dial, giving it a quick test. Sure enough, propane seeps out.

"What if this doesn't work?" she asks.

"Then it doesn't work. We have to do something, though. We don't have time to look for the key to the back door. He'll smell this and be busy running around trying to figure out where it's coming from that he won't pay attention to the basement. We'll open it, duck into the dining room, then out the other side to the front door. With any luck, he'll figure out it's coming from the living room. He'll be in there trying to block the vent and will have no clue of our escape."

"What if there's a flame?"

I pause. "Why would there be a flame?"

"I don't know. I'm just asking."

"Then...the house explodes." I throw my arms up. "I don't know what to tell you. What else are we going to do?"

She takes a deep breath, handing me a large rag. "Tie this around your face." With a nod, I do, and she does the same.

We share one last determined look.

Before I talk myself out of this decision, I twist the knob on the tank. Gas hisses out. Lifting on my toes, I shove the small unit in as far as it will go to the right, propping it in the curve of the duct work. Carefully, I release it, and it stays in place.

Martha tears off several more strips of duct tape that I use to seal the remaining hole with.

In the monitor, her ex is currently examining the crease of the steel door. He wedges a butter knife into the top and slowly trails it down the right side, looking for hinges I guess. He does the left as well.

With the rags tied around our faces and each with a screwdriver in our hand for a weapon, we walk up the steps, ready at the door to make our move.

Her ex pauses, stepping away from the door. Lifting his head, he sniffs. *Here we go.*

A glance at the vent shows the duct tape is still holding tight, preventing the gas from leaking back down into here.

On the giant screen, we watch her ex pace the kitchen. He stops at the stove, checking the knobs, realizing that it is electric.

He sniffs the air again, coughing as he hurries over to wedge open the kitchen windows.

Come on. Come on. Go into the living room.

Quickly, he races into the eating area, wedging those windows open as well.

"Can we go out a window?" I ask.

Martha shakes her head. "No. I had security ones installed. They open a quarter of the way. And they have screens. It was supposed to keep someone from coming in."

Or going out, in our case.

"The front door is our only option," she says.

Another glance at the vent down here shows the duct tape still securely in place. He is getting all the gas.

On the monitor, her ex stumbles into the living room, going straight toward those windows.

"Now!" I push Martha toward the keypad.

Her fingers race over the numbers.

On the monitor, he wedges open a window, pausing to gulp fresh air.

Back down here, the keypad's not working.

"What is going on?" I move in next to Martha.

"I don't know." She punches the numbers again. "It's not working."

This is not happening. "Okay, take a deep breath. What are the numbers?"

"Zero-eight-zero-five-seven-one." She says each number as she presses it. The light on the keypad stays red. "See? It's not working."

Back on the monitor, her ex steps away from the living room window. Slowly, he turns, studying something on the floor.

Oh, crap. "I think he's figured it out."

Martha coughs. I look over to the vent. A tiny bit of duct tape has peeled loose. I race down the basement steps, and grabbing the roll of duct tape, I hurry up the ladder. Tearing off a strip of tape, I slam it over the vent. I repeat, doubling up on the layers.

"It's not working," Martha cries. She punches the numbers again. The steady red light now rapidly blinks. "Oh, no."

"What?" I snap.

"That means we've timed out. I can't try the code again for an hour. It's a safety feature."

My response grinds out, each word laced with irritability. "Of. Course. It. Is."

Her ex hurries from the living room back into the kitchen. He opens the cabinet beneath the sink and brings out a small bucket with rags. Turning away from the camera angle, he raises his ski mask, layers several rags over his nose and mouth, then lowers the ski mask back into place.

Sliding the gun from the back of his waist band, he holds it up so we can see it in the camera. Next from under the kitchen sink, he retrieves a fire extinguisher that he takes into the living room. From the sectional sofa, he selects a decorative pillow. He moves as far away as possible into the archway that leads back into the hall.

Martha's words come back to me. *What if there's a flame?*

My eyes widen. He wouldn't.

My gaze bounces over to Martha whose eyes freeze wide as she also stares at what he's doing.

"No-no-no-no-no." I yank the duct tape from the vent and shove my arm up inside. Gas travels across the ceiling of the basement, making me woozy.

Coughing, Martha staggers down the steps.

"Get those blankets from the shelves!" My hand latches onto the tank. I jerk it back down, quickly rotate the knob off, and stumble from the step ladder.

My legs tremble. My throat seizes with a deep cough.

Martha snaps a large blanket open.

On the monitor, her ex aims the gun at the vent. The stuffing from it explodes. The pillow does nothing to silence it. Down here, the shot reverberates through the air, followed by a whooshing sound. Flames shoot from the vent. A hot blue cloud crawls the ceiling.

I throw myself at Martha. We drop to the floor. She covers us both with the blanket. The row of bulbs along the ceiling explodes. Glass showers us.

Then, silence.

For a few seconds, we stay huddled under the blanket, both panting for air.

"Are you okay?" she asks.

"I think so. You?"

"Yes."

Carefully, I peek out from under the covers. A smokey haze surrounds us. One lone bulb survived, casting the basement in a flickering uneven glow. Black stretches from the vent to crawl the ceiling. But other than the glass now littering the floor, the walls and shelves stayed intact. On the monitor, similar soot extends from the living room vent just a few inches outward. Her ex sprays the fire extinguisher on one dancing flame. It dies.

We got the worst down here.

Lowering the rag from my nose, I test the air. All is fine. We get to our feet.

There is no broom, so I use the blanket to sweep the glass over into the corner behind the beanbag.

"Look at him, all cocky," Martha snaps.

In the monitor, her ex moves from room to room in satisfying slow strides, closing back and locking the windows. In the kitchen, he pauses to flip us a bird in the camera.

Though he can't see me, I flip him one right back.

She said he wasn't bright, but he's proving otherwise.

8

Friday 3 a.m.

MARTHA SAGS INTO THE BEANBAG. Her head falls back and her eyes close. She looks drained. But I'm not. Nervous energy drives my movements as I more closely inspect the contents of the shelves.

"What are you doing?" she asks, her voice as tired as she looks.

"Brainstorming." I open the box labeled OLD STUFF, finding a rotary phone, a stained stuffed animal, a friendship bracelet, a pink striped scrapbook labeled MY LIFE, an old ballerina jewelry box, a zip lock bag full of foreign coins—

"That's private." Martha sits up. "Put it back."

My eyebrows shoot up, but I comply.

I turn to look at her. "Why do you think the code didn't work?"

"Maybe he cut the wires."

"No." I point to the monitor that shows the exterior view of the door. "The keypad out there is still in place. He didn't remove it and cut the wires."

"Then perhaps he killed the electricity."

"No." Again, I point to the monitor. "Electricity's on."

"I don't know what to tell you. Maybe something happened when he took the door off or jammed that butter knife into the seam."

"Yeah, maybe..." I look back at the screen, right as car lights come into view. Through the porch-mounted camera, I watch as a vehicle pulls past this house to park at the Airbnb beside. "Oh my God, someone just pulled in next door."

Martha's ex hurries into the living room, double-checking the blinds are closed. He parts them, peering out at the magnolia trees and the Airbnb beyond.

The car parks. The driver and passenger doors open. A man and a young girl get out. They open the trunk of their car, each grabbing an armful of supplies. Hopefully, that means they are going to be here a while. In tired, groggy strides, the girl heaves a duffel bag and plastic bag full of groceries across the yard and up to the house. The man beeps his car lock and then follows. They disappear inside.

The camera's current angle gives a view of the small driveway, the porch, and the front door. It's three in the morning. I doubt they're going to do anything other than crawl in bed. I'm just about to turn away when the front door reopens and the man appears. He lights a cigarette and stands smoking, looking out over the woods that front our small street.

With the mouse, I click the "Talk" button on that camera. "Hello?"

The man doesn't look over.

I raise my voice. "Hello?"

He still doesn't move.

It's a good fifty yards away. I try again. "HELLO?"

"You should stop," Martha says. "You know who can hear you."

My gaze flicks over to one of the interior views that shows her ex standing at the front door, his ear pressed to the wood panels.

I let go of the "Talk" button. I don't want to risk that he'll rip the camera out of its mount and disable it.

A good solid moment beats by before he turns away to tread the hall back to the kitchen. I press the "Talk" button again. A green light flashes across the porch.

A new idea forms.

I do it again, and again a green light flashes.

Again, and again the light.

I keep clicking the "Talk" button, flashing the green light.

On-off.

On-off.

On-off.

Curious, Martha gets to her feet and comes to stand beside me. The camera light flashes, illuminating the early morning hours. Still smoking the cigarette, the man finally glances over.

"Come on. Come on." I keep clicking the "Talk" button in a jerky on-off pattern. Martha leans into me, her attention fastened on the man.

The man turns fully to face Martha's house.

"Yes. Yes. Yes." I keep flashing the camera light.

The man walks to the end of the porch.

"Please. Please." I keep flashing, faster and faster.

The man leans forward, really looking now.

Suddenly, the monitor goes black.

"No!" I jab the "Talk" button. "Hello, are you there?" I smack the screen. "What's going on? Where's our power?" I look at Martha. "What happened?"

"I don't know."

Frantically, I check the cables. Everything looks connected. I click the mouse. *No*.

Martha touches my shoulder. "It was a good idea."

Shoving away, I pace a tight circle. "This is not happening. He saw the light. Did you see it? He saw the light"

She nods. "I'm sorry."

The urge to cry overpowers me. Instead, I yell. I kick the wall. I yell again. "THE MAN SAW. HE SAW."

The monitor flicks back on.

I race over, nearly knocking Martha to the side. My gaze flies across the camera views. But the man went inside. He's gone.

I give in, and I cry. *We're never getting out of here.*

9

Friday 4:03 a.m.

MARTHA SITS ON THE BEANBAG, nibbling the inside of her cheek, watching her ex punch random codes into the keypad. "What an idiot. He just keeps timing the system out."

I stand staring at the shelves, mentally reviewing each item and how it might get us out of here. I've been so focused on getting through that door that I haven't brainstormed other ways. So far, the closest we've gotten is when we almost made contact with the man next door.

Making contact...

The laptop down here has no connectivity. Her security system is doing what it is supposed to do—keep the bad guy out. But there has to be a way to reach an outside source.

Forget technology. Go old school.

The Lady Next Door

The box labeled OLD STUFF catches my attention again. "There's a rotary phone in that box. Does it work?"

She shrugs.

"Well, will you get it? You freaked out when you saw me riffling through it earlier."

With a sigh, she pushes out of the beanbag and goes about slowly dragging the step ladder over to the shelves. I don't know what her problem is, but I feel like I'm the only one focused on getting out of here.

While she retrieves the phone, I grab a hammer and flat head screwdriver from the toolbox. I take both along with the flashlight up the steps to the door. A sturdy wood frame brackets in the steel door with a finished dry wall on both sides followed by brick. The keypad sits to the left. I put the flat head against the dry wall a few inches away from the keypad and give it a good whack. The blade sinks in, creating a tiny hole.

I do it again, making the hole a little wider.

And again, yet wider.

"What are you doing?" Martha comes up the steps.

"Over at my house, all the wiring runs next to the doorways. I'm hoping your place is the same way."

"Okay, but what are you doing?"

"Just watch the monitor. Make sure he can't hear me." Another hard whack. The hole gets bigger.

Though I told Martha to watch the screen, I hesitate, looking myself. Her ex has stopped punching in random numbers and is staring at the blinking red light. Maybe he'll figure out that he's timed out the system.

One more time with the hammer and screwdriver. Now the hole is about two inches wide. Using the flashlight, I peer inside, seeing insulation and wiring. With my fingers, I work more of the drywall loose, making the hole jagged and bigger. Gently, I pull several cords through the insulation and out of the hole.

With a triumphant grin, I look over at Martha. "We are going to connect that old phone."

"I don't have landline service."

"Yes, you do. Around here, it comes standard with the internet." Handing off the flashlight, I race down the steps and over to the toolbox to get wire strippers.

When I was in high school, I served on the Tech Team as part of the Drama Club. For the most part, it was just a way for me to earn an elective credit I needed to graduate. But it also taught me things like stripping wires, reconnecting, and soldering.

I draw on that long-ago knowledge now as I hightail it back up the steps. The phone cord is coated in white and bigger than the others. It only takes me a few seconds to strip the plastic coating and sever it in half. I'm not entirely sure how to do this, but as long as I match up colors, I would think I'm heading in the right direction.

Martha stands one step below me holding the flashlight and rotary phone. The old cable that used to connect to a wall outlet is wrapped loosely around the base. I unwrap it, finding it to be fairly long, maybe even five feet. I double-check it's still firmly seated into the base, then I repeat, stripping the plastic coating and severing the cord. Both the phone and wall cables have red, brown, and green wires, but the phone also has yellow.

The flashlight goes out.

"Sorry," Martha mumbles, flicking it back on.

I match up the red, brown, and green, twisting them together, and leave the yellow dangling. I test the connection. It doesn't work.

The flashlight goes out.

"Sorry," Martha mumbles, flicking it back on.

I take the extra yellow and combine it with the red. I test the connection. It doesn't work.

The flashlight goes out.

"Sorry," Martha mumbles, flicking it back on.

I take the extra yellow and combine it with the green. I raise the receiver to my ear and I cannot believe a dial tone comes through. "It works!"

The flashlight goes out.

"Sorry," Martha mumbles, flicking it back on.

"What the hell, Martha?"

"I'm sorry. The battery must be dying."

I assume calling nine-one-one works the same on a rotary phone. Poking my index finger in the nine-hole, I rotate the dial clockwise. It click-click-clicks counter-clockwise back into place. I repeat with one—click, click, click— followed by the second one—click, click, click.

"How do you know how to use one of these?" she asks.

"I don't know. I just do."

"I don't even know why I have this. I've never used it. Maybe it belonged to a grandparent or something."

An operator picks up. My heart leaps. "Nine-one-one. What is your emergency?"

The flashlight goes out.

The connection clicks off.

"No!"

Martha slaps the flashlight, but this time it doesn't flick back on. I double-check the twisted wires the best I can in the dimly-lit basement, undoing them, redoing them. I check for a dial tone, once again hearing it. My index finger fumbles with the rotary, going through the slow process of once again dialing.

"Nine-one-one. What is your emergency?"

The line dies.

Desperately, I try again. Undoing and redoing the wires, rotary dialing nine-one-one. But no more dial tone comes.

"Goddammit!" I rip the dead flashlight from Martha's hand and I hurl it down into the basement. It lands and rolls, flicking back to life.

I look at Martha who calmly stands beside me, her fingers lightly grasping the base. "I'm sorry it didn't work. It was a good idea, though."

This time I don't cry or yell, I full-on scream my head off.

10

Friday 4:22 a.m.

IN THE MONITOR, her ex has moved on to removing the keypad.

"What happens if he takes that off?" I ask.

"Well, if he cuts the wires then we'll be stuck down here."

"Fabulous."

Stepping away from the keypad, he moves toward the archway that leads into the hall. Frozen in place, he stares at the front door.

My gaze darts across the large monitor, trying to figure out what he's looking at. I suck in a breath when I do.

It's Popeye.

He's on the front porch clawing and barking at the door. What the hell? He must have dug under my back fence and followed my scent. I press the "Talk" button. "Popeye, go home. Go home now!"

His head cocks. He looks around.

"Popeye, you've got to go home. Now, boy. Now."

His little brown eyes lift. He looks up at the camera.

"You're a good boy. But you have to go home."

The front door opens. Martha's ex comes into view.

"Go home!" I yell.

"Well, what do we have here?" It's the first time I've heard him speak. Through the ski mask, his voice comes deep and gravely. "Come on in, Doggy."

"Popeye, no. Go home!"

My dog pauses, probably thrown off by the man in the ski mask mixed with my voice coming from the unknown.

"Buddy, you've got to go home," I plead.

His tail wags. He races into the house. The door closes.

"No," I moan. "This is not happening."

Popeye sniffs me out, going first to the kitchen, then into the eating area, upstairs, then back down to the living room, finally coming back into the kitchen and stopping at the basement door.

Our intruder doesn't move from his spot in the hallway. He simply watches my dog roam the house.

Tail wagging, Popeye claws at the steel door.

Martha's ex stalks the length of the hall, coming into the kitchen. He steps right up beside my dog, roughly bumping into him. Popeye loses his balance, glancing up at the human in confusion.

I press the button. "Leave him alone."

Popeye hears my voice and barks.

Her ex slams his fist into the steel door. My dog jumps.

Eyes glued to the screen, my thoughts spin. Letting go of

the "talk" button, I look over at Martha. "Will he hurt my dog?"

She doesn't respond.

"Martha?"

"Yes, probably."

Roughly, I grab her arm. "Are you sure you punched in the right code before?"

"Yes."

"Try it again."

"Then he'll get in."

"I don't care. I need my dog. Try it again."

"I can't. It's still timed out from all of his tamperings."

A glance up the steps shows the usual steady red light, blinking, indicating Martha is right. It's timed out.

On the screen, her ex shuffles around the kitchen, corralling Popeye who tucks his tail and allows it. He doesn't have an alpha bone in his doggy body.

I click the "Talk" button. "Does it make you feel like a real man to bully a tiny helpless creature? You're pathetic."

Pulling the gun from his waistband, he squats down, letting my dog sniff it. Then he points it right between Popeye's brown eyes.

My heart stops.

The poor little guy loses his bladder as he backs into the kitchen corner.

Our intruder stands up. He writes something on a piece of paper and holds it up.

OPEN THE DOOR.

My finger jabs unsteadily into the "Talk" button. "We can't. You timed it out with all your tampering. See that blinking red light? We can't open it until it turns solid red."

Tears push from my eyes. Swiping them away, I stare at Popeye. "You're a good boy," I say, my words trembling. "You're a good, good, sweet boy."

He whines.

"Please, just wait." My voice breaks. "As soon as we're allowed, we'll punch in the *right* code." I look over at Martha. "Right?"

She doesn't respond.

"Right?" I grind out.

"Right," she murmurs.

Her maniacal ex once again points the gun at Popeye. He holds up one gloved finger.

What the hell?

He holds up another gloved finger.

Oh my God.

A third gloved finger starts to go up—

Covering my face, I turn away. I can't watch this.

Martha grabs my arm. "Look."

I don't.

"No, seriously. Look."

Hesitantly, I turn back. She's pointing to a cop standing on the front porch. He looks fresh-from-the-academy young. Behind him on the street sits his squad car. My finger jams down on the "Talk" button. "Help!"

The cop doesn't even stir.

"Help!"

Again, he doesn't stir.

I double-check I'm clicking the correct button. "Help!"

Nothing.

I look over to Martha. "What's going on? Why isn't this working? It was working a few seconds ago."

"No clue."

Through the peep hole, her ex checks to see who is on

the porch. Quickly, he takes his ski mask off. The hallway camera gives me a shot of the back of his shaved dark head. It's the first time I've seen him. To the right of the front door sits a decorative potted plant. He stashes the gun in it before opening the front door.

I press "Talk" again. "Help!"

But again, the cop doesn't blink.

Their voices filter though...

"Good evening, Officer," Martha's ex says, his voice deep like before but this time I make out an Australian accent. "Or should I say, good morning?" He chuckles. "May I help you?"

The porch camera shows me the crown of his head. I still haven't seen his face. "He's Australian?"

"No," Martha says. "That's fake."

The young cop speaks, "Sir, we received a nine-one-one call from this residence. Twice, both hang-ups. Is everything okay? We have the owner listed as one Martha Allen."

"Yes, that's my girlfriend. She'll be here tomorrow or the next." He opens the door wide, letting the young cop see the pristine hallway. Too bad he can't see the living room with the singed vent or the kitchen with the removed door. "She just bought the place. Sorry about that nine-one-one call. That's on me. I hooked up a landline. It has quick dial numbers. I accidentally pressed the emergency one. I didn't realize it went through."

Popeye comes down the hallway. He pushes past about to make a run for it when the cop grabs his collar. "Hey there, little dude."

Leaning down, Martha's ex takes hold. "Where're you going, silly Popeye?"

I hate that he knows my dog's name.

He tugs him back into the house, using his leg to scoot

Popeye further in. My dog takes off, leaping the stairs up to the second floor. He barks, and barks, and barks.

"Dang beagles get a scent, and they are off." Martha's ex lets out a good-natured chuckle. "Anything else?"

Smiling a little, the cop shakes his head. "I'll leave you be. Have a good rest of your evening-slash-morning. And be careful with those emergency numbers."

"Will do."

With that, the cop walks back to the awaiting squad car.

Our intruder closes the door, but before he turns around, he puts the ski mask back on. He knows where the cameras are and how to avoid showing his face. With the gun retrieved from the decorative potted plant, he takes the stairs up to the second floor in search of my dog.

I try one more time. "Help!" But the cop still doesn't hear. He doesn't even glance up at the house as he gets back into his car.

I note the keypad has already gone back to steady red. That was sooner than an hour. "It's ready. Martha, it's ready. Go punch in the code."

She begins convulsing.

What the...

I try to catch her but her body bucks from my arms as she falls to the floor. She's having a seizure, but I don't know what from. I race over to the shelves, frantically searching for anything to put into her mouth. There's an instructional manual in the toolbox to a drill. It only takes me a few seconds to wedge it into her jaw. I help her ride out the spasms until she finally quiets.

Her body shudders. It tenses, then relaxes. A sigh leaves her. But she's not coherent. I remove the manual from her mouth, roll her onto her side, and check for a pulse.

It's stronger than I expect. That's good.

With a shiver, her knees move slightly, tucking in. She's coming to. Her lashes flutter, barely opening, but she doesn't make eye contact with me.

I leave her where she is. She'll be fine.

Back on the monitor, I spy her crazy ex upstairs on his hands and knees trying to get Popeye out from under the bed.

I leap up the steps and closing my eyes, I rewind this night to when we first escaped down here. Martha punched in a code. I visualize her finger moving. It wasn't zero-eight-zero-five-seven-one, like she said, it was zero-eight-zero-five-seven-zero. There wasn't a one on the end. In her panic, she must have mixed numbers up.

Holding my breath, I do the code I think it is, praying I'm right.

0-8-0-5-7-0

Quietly, the door opens.

Son of a bitch. It worked. Martha's still curled on her side, her back to me. At the top of the steps are all of the tools I've used. Picking up the hammer, I move into the kitchen.

In my socks, I race down the hall to the stairwell. At the base of the steps, I look up. Which one was the squeaky one? Either number four or five, I think. I climb, stretching wide and skipping those two steps.

It works.

Mumbled cursing tumbles through the air. Popeye's nails scrape across the floor. With the hammer held high, I tiptoe into the master suite.

"You are not worth all of this trouble," our intruder grumbles, his body halfway under the canopy bed as he struggles to get my dog.

Popeye growls.

If there was ever a time that I wish my dog was a biter, it's now. But he's not. He flees, not fights. Which is exactly what he's doing under the bed.

I come to a stop at a pair of black boots. I survey our intruder's calves, the back of his legs, his butt—all covered in dark cargo pants.

"I swear to God, I'm not going to shoot you," he says, his voice deep and muffled from the ski mask. "No, I'm going to tear your toenails out one by one and let your mommy watch."

My hand tightens around the hammer. I swing it up, and with every bit of muscle I have, I deliver a ferocious blow to his ankle.

A bone crunches.

He yells. His body jerks.

Not a second of reprieve is given as I deliver another blow, this one to his other ankle.

Another bone crunches.

Desperation has him scrambling under the tall bed. He emerges out the other side, grabbing the gun from his waistband as he does. I stalk him, kicking the weapon. It thuds and slides across the floor.

His gloved hand comes up. He flips me off. "Fuck. You."

I deliver a vicious kick to his ribs.

He yells.

Once again, I lift the hammer. The next blow comes with more force and savagery than the others. There is no mercy as I pummel his torso, ignoring his frantic scream.

Hurling myself up and back down, I deliver the last, slamming hard into his jaw. Sweat flies from my brow. If I were standing by watching this, I would be horror-stricken.

He stills.

Chest heaving, I hover over his unconscious body. I fall

The Lady Next Door

to my knees. The hammer clambers to the floor. Popeye races out from under the bed and into my arms. I hold him close, burying my face in his fur. The horrifying scene tears through me. I sob.

I'm not sure how much time goes by, but when I finally get myself in control, I look at Martha's ex. He's breathing, just barely. His ski mask came halfway off during our fight. Something about his profile—the lips, the dark stubble—nudges at me.

Crawling over, I grab the mask and yank it off.

I try to speak, but my mouth is dry. I swallow. One word scrapes my throat. "Quinn?"

From behind, Martha speaks. "This did not turn out the way I planned."

Then, she jabs me with a needle.

11

Friday, 3:00 p.m.

My lips move. Martha leans in, putting her ear down next to my mouth.

"What is it?" she asks.

I try to summon enough strength to speak, but my breath comes hard. Something is wrong with me. "Please..."

"Please what?"

"Help me."

"Maybe we should wait and see what happens."

I swallow, licking my dry lips. My reply comes breathy, almost inaudible. "Something's wrong."

"I know what you need."

She opens a case. Plastic crinkles. "You're the nurse not me, but I've watched enough YouTube to know what to do. If I mess up, feel free to correct me."

I try to form words, but I'm weak. I thought she said that she was a nurse.

She ties tubing around my arm. She thumps my veins. "According to YouTube, I'm supposed to go in at a shallow angle."

Something pricks the inside of my arm.

MY EYES FLUTTER OPEN. White. Blurry white—it's all I see.

I squeeze my eyes shut, then reopen them. A row of too-bright bulbs glares back at me. Martha moves into my line of sight. Her lips purse, then she smiles. "Hi."

I try to sit up, but nausea rolls through me. My head is killing me.

My dry tongue works around my mouth. "What's going on?"

"Try not to move." She puts a cup of water to my lips. Greedily, I drink.

My eyes close again. My head sinks into a pillow. I groan. Feeling returns to my body in sections of warmth. She moves away, fiddling with my ankles. I dig around in my brain, trying to remember what happened. Someone broke into her home. We escaped to the basement. Popeye showed up. So did a cop. Our intruder—

Quinn. It was my ex-husband, Quinn.

And I killed him.

Or at least I think I did.

No, he was still breathing. Wasn't he?

My eyes fly open. I struggle to sit up, but my arms and legs won't move. I'm tied down. It's then I realize I'm hooked to an IV. "Wh-what's going on?"

Gently, Martha squeezes my lower leg. "You're okay. Just be still."

I struggle again to sit up, but my restraints keep me

firmly in place. "Martha, what is going on? Why am I tied down? And what are you giving me?"

She moves into my line of sight again. "Stop moving around. Those zip ties will break your skin. And I'm giving you saline. That's all."

"Where's Quinn?"

"No worries. I took care of him." She chuckles. "It's hard digging a grave."

I struggle one last time to sit up. The zip ties bite into my skin. I cringe.

I'm on a twin-sized bed, tied to four posts, in a room about twenty by twenty with brick walls and a concrete floor. In the left corner, a walkway leads into a bathroom with no door. Straight ahead sits a flat-screen TV mounted to the wall. To the right is a closed door that I assume leads out of this room. One night stand holds a stack of historical romance novels plus an open milk crate filled with Larabars, organic juice boxes, snack bags of dried fruits and nuts, and various other things.

I recognize that crate. It was on her bottom shelf in the basement.

The basement…

It also had brick walls and a concrete floor.

"Are we in your basement?"

"Yes, on the other side of the shelves." Smiling, she waves her arms around. "The previous owners made this for visiting family. I installed the hidden wall and shelves, making this perfect for my needs. Or rather our needs. Do you like it?" She points to the open crate and the stack of novels. "All your favorites. I was going to do so much more with this place, but Quinn 'broke in' much sooner than he was supposed to. I think he got excited when I told him you were coming over for Chinese food and wine. Though I already feel like I know you inside and out, I still wanted to *actually* get to know you before I moved you in here. But leave it to Quinn to jump the gun."

I don't know what is going on. She is making no sense. "What day is it? What time is it?"

"It's Friday, three in the afternoon."

I came over here Thursday night for Chinese food. The last time I looked at the security monitor, the clock read 4:22 a.m. I went upstairs. I attacked Quinn. Martha stuck me with a needle. "What did you give me?"

"I already told you, I'm giving you saline to hydrate you."

"No, before. The needle."

"Oh, ketamine. You've been out roughly ten hours. I was getting worried. I thought it would only knock you out for a couple of hours at best. That's why I decided to hook you up to an IV." She grins. "It's my first one." She nods to it taped to my inner arm. "How did I do?"

"How did you get me down here?"

"I tried a fireman's hold, but that didn't work as I thought. So I put you on a blanket and drug you down here. It worked so well I did it with Quinn as well."

"What did you do with him?"

"I did all this for you, ya know."

"What did you do with him?"

"I put him out of his misery." She chuckles. "You did a number on him with that hammer."

"Where's his body?"

"I buried him in the woods across the street. It's amazing how his death has already cut an invisible tie. I'm released. Don't you also feel it? Oh, and I was careful. No one saw me. You're right. This is the best street. So private. It's perfect really. I also went over to your house and got things for you and Popeye." She laughs. "He is such a good little boy."

"You can't just keep me here. Someone will know. Someone will come looking. My dad—"

"No. You said yourself you rarely if ever talk to him."

"My job. They—"

"Nope. That's all covered as well. I called the hospital and spoke with your supervisor. I pretended to be your doctor. You were in an accident with your father while visiting him in Florida. You're in the hospital down there, recovering. Your supervisor was super understanding. I told her I'd keep her in the loop." Smiling ecstatically, she straightens up. "I've been so eager for you to wake up. Are you hungry?"

This is not happening. Am I in some sort of nightmare? I have to be. I need to wake up.

"Are you hungry?" she repeats.

"Take this IV out of my arm. Now."

Frowning, she leans in close, studying my pupils. "You should probably rest, I think. Or maybe I should make you eat. What do you think? You're the nurse."

"Martha—"

"Rest, I think." She nods, once.

Around her neck dangles a key. She takes it off as she turns away, crossing over to the door. She dims the lights in the room. "I'll see you later." Then with that, she's gone.

12

Saturday 6 a.m.

THE KEY RATTLES in the door. It opens. Softly, almost sweetly, Martha laughs as she steps through. Wearing white scrubs with cartoon characters, she holds up a pack of baby wipes.

Those are my scrubs.

"Good morning." She comes up beside me. Her fingers hover over the needle taped to my arm. "Shall we take this out?"

"Yes."

With a nod, she peels the tape away. A large bruise has formed under and around the needle where she likely poked me several times to get the IV in. Hell, she probably went straight through my vein. She walks into the bathroom, opens a cabinet above the toilet, and comes back with a small first aid kit. From inside she selects gauze and tape.

Carefully, she slides the needle out. I wince. Blood

swells. She presses gauze to it, holding it firmly. "I trust you slept well?"

"I didn't sleep at all."

Her bottom lip pokes out. "I'm sorry." She checks under the gauze, seeing it's still bleeding.

"It's fine," I tell her. "Just secure it with tape."

She does and sitting on the bed beside me, she takes out a baby wipe.

"Martha, you can't keep me in h—"

"You're exactly like I thought you'd be." She wipes my face.

"Excuse me?"

Martha concentrates on a spot near my ear. "The way Quinn described you."

"How do you know my ex-husband?"

With gentle fingers, she pinches my chin and moves my head left. "We're lovers. Or rather, *were* lovers. He talked about you all the time. At first, it bothered me. But then...I couldn't get enough. I needed to see."

"Needed to see what?"

"You." She smiles. "I needed to see my Quinn's obsession."

Her Quinn?

"I mean your hair is different but everything else is like he described." She selects another baby wipe and pushing up the sleeve of my tee, she cleans my right arm. "I wondered what you had that I didn't."

"Nothing. I don't ha—"

"Oh, of course." She waves me off. "I was wondering how I was going to 'meet' you and put all of this in motion. Lucky for me, you walked right in my front door." She throws that wipe away and selects another. "I know everything about you—favorite food, wine, hobbies, clothes, college, job, family. I even know what soap you like." She leans in. "I *am* you."

Oh, shit.

"And what, you convinced Quinn to be part of this kidnapping-his-ex plot?"

She moves around to the other side of the bed. Pushing up that sleeve, she wipes my left arm. "This room was his fantasy. So was the break-in." She lowers her voice, imitating Quinn. "'I'd love to break into the bitch's house and terrorize her, then lock her in a room and teach her a lesson.' I didn't know what kind of lesson he wanted to teach you, but I was curious enough to see. I mean eventually, I wanted you all to myself, but I was willing to let him play. For a little while at least."

I feel sick.

She selects another baby wipe, and nudging into my arm pits, she cleans them. "Despite all of his trash talking, I know you're kind and intelligent. My Quinn would have never married anybody else. All this right here? We're honoring his memory."

"My father, my job, they may not initially realize I'm missing, but eventually they'll figure it out. Not to mention Quinn. He's from a big family."

"Oh, I've already figured all of that out. I sent a mass email to them from him. He's hopped a sailboat and will be back when he's back. You know that's a very Quinn thing to do."

That's true. His wanderlust is one of the things that attracted me to him. Unfortunately, it took me entirely too long to figure out he was a maniac.

With my arm pits done, she lifts my tee and does my stomach and chest. "Of course, with you, it's only your dad, who you rarely talk to." She looks genuinely thrilled. "Just think of all the time we'll have to truly get to know each other."

Despite this insane situation I'm now in, my stomach growls. I hate that it does.

Laughing, she leans in to talk to it. "I hear you. I'll give you something in a few minutes. I made one of your favorites."

More baby wipes come and go as she takes my socks off, cleans my feet, and lowers my leggings to wipe both legs.

Wait a minute, I'm wearing an adult diaper.

She put it on me when I was knocked out on ketamine. I should be bothered by this, but what the diaper signifies disturbs me more.

Though her touch has been clinical, when she reaches for the diaper, I stop her. "I would prefer you not."

"Okay, I'll respect that." She pulls my leggings back up, puts my socks on, and gathers the used wipes. Rolling the IV stand, she walks to the door. "Don't go anywhere," she says, giggling at her stupid joke. "Be right back."

Her slippers shuffle across the basement floor and up the steps.

Lifting my head, I survey the zip ties around my ankles. I pull at them, wincing at the pinch against my skin.

I need to go to the bathroom. Bad. I'm sure as hell not going in this diaper.

Her feet tread the steps, coming back down into the basement. She reappears in the doorway, carrying a tray. "I made you tofu scramble with black bean sausage. Your favorite breakfast."

"How do you know that's my favorite?"

Chuckling, Martha shakes her head, like that's the silliest question of all time. She once again sits beside me on the bed. With a fork, she cuts a chunk of sausage and holds it up to my lips. Reluctantly, I open my mouth and eat it. She gives me tofu scramble next made with vegan mayonnaise. I hate tofu scramble with vegan mayonnaise. I hate vegan mayonnaise period. I prefer Dijon mustard, always.

Yet, I chew and swallow. "You faked that seizure, didn't you? And the panic attack? Not to mention all the problems with the code not working, the flashlight conveniently going out, the laptop losing power, and the 'Talk' button failing to connect when the cop arrived."

"Mm." She shrugs. "You did come up with some great ideas, though, very *Panic Room* of you."

I'm an idiot.

"I wanted to talk to you about something." She gives me another bite of black bean sausage. "It's ridiculous. Just a minor thought."

"Regarding?"

"Veganism." The one-word bursts from her mouth.

I wait.

"It's just when I went over to your house yesterday, I noticed you have cheese crackers in your pantry. If you're vegan, you don't eat dairy. Cheese is dairy."

She holds a fork full of tofu scramble to my lips. I eat because I don't know what to say.

"If you're a vegan, then be vegan. Don't be a sometimes one."

I'm not sure why, but this odd conversation amuses me.

"What?" she asks.

"Nothing. I just wasn't expecting you to lecture me on eating."

Lifting the fork to my lips, she gives me the last chunk of sausage. I eat. She follows that with a bite of tofu. I eat that as well. A glob of mayonnaise-laden scramble plops onto my shirt. Sighing, she dabs it up with a cloth napkin. One more bite and I'm done. She places the napkin on the plate.

Another sigh leaves her, this one agitated. "Well, did you like it?"

"Sure, I guess."

"What's that mean?"

"I eat my scramble with Dijon mustard, not vegan mayonnaise." I shrug. "I guess you don't know me as well as you think you do." I'm antagonizing her, but I don't care.

Her cheeks redden. Flustered, she stands. "W-well. Fine. Next time I'll remember."

Carrying the tray, she almost trips over her own feet getting to the door.

"Martha?"

She pauses, her back to me.

"I need to go to the bathroom."

Slowly, she turns. Her red, flustered cheeks fade into a shrewd look that meets mine. "Then go."

Now it's my turn to be flustered. "What, here in the bed?"

"Yep." With that, she closes and locks the door.

13

Saturday 12 p.m.

THE MORNING GOES BY. I do everything I can to take my mind off of my bathroom needs. Hell, I even count sheep and recite the alphabet backward. Multiple times.

When the door opens, it jars me. Martha walks in, pausing when she notices my eyes were closed. "I didn't realize you were taking a nap." On the wall a dimmer switch has stayed on this whole time, providing soft illumination. She reaches for it. "Should I lower this to dark and leave you be?"

"I prefer it on." With no windows, it's the only light. If she lowers the dimmer, it will cast the entire room black.

Lifting my head off the pillow, I look at the floor, hoping to see Popeye. "How's my dog?"

"He's fine."

"When can I see him?"

"To be determined." From behind her back, she brings out several journals, all leather, in multiple colors.

They belong to me, dating back to my teen years. Writing my thoughts is something I don't do every day or even every week, but at least monthly—when I feel the need. Some people talk through their thoughts, decisions, worries…I've always written mine.

"I went back over to your house. Figured I better check your mail, scroll through your inbox, etcetera. You really should password protect your laptop."

From here on out I will.

"It was mostly junk. I logged into your cell phone account since Quinn destroyed your actual phone. You had one voice mail from your boss, telling you to take whatever time you need. They have your shifts covered. Your email had a couple of reminders of automatic payments coming up. I trust you have enough money in your bank account?"

"I'm fine."

"Good. Is there anything else you can think of that I need to take care of?"

"Why? Exactly how long do you plan on keep—"

"Quinn never told me about these." Excitement prances through her eyes as she holds up the journals, simultaneously dancing on the balls of her feet.

"Because they're private."

"Oh, you. Private-schmivate. You forget we're each other's doppelgänger. That means we share everything. They were right there in the drawer of your nightstand. Who would've guessed?"

She thumbs through a navy-blue one with hearts drawn on the front in sharpie. That's the very first journal I ever kept.

"I peeked at the first few pages." Her voice softens. "I'm

so sorry your mother left. I mean, I knew, of course. But to read the pain..." Pressing the journal to her breast, she looks at me, like she's seeing me for the first time. "So much about you makes sense now."

"Martha, I have to go to the bathroom."

"I know," she says, her voice still soft.

With that, she once again strolls from the room.

14

Saturday 6 p.m.

I SHOULD FEEL HUMILIATED that I'm lying here in urine and feces. But I don't. I'm angry. Furious.

As I've done multiple times now, I tug at the zip ties around my wrists and ankles. The plastic cuts in, coating my skin with fresh blood. I wince. The smell of my diaper permeates the room in a horrendously strong stench.

I haven't showered since I came over here for Chinese food and wine. That was two days ago now. I know this because the flat screen mounted on the wall directly in front of me flashes every so often with the day and time.

Like an annoying reminder.

The door opens. Martha enters carrying a tray of food and a glass of water.

"I'm not hungry."

Her nose wrinkles. "Phew, you stink."

"You have got to let me up. I'm serious. This is a health issue. You can't leave me here in this diaper. I'm going to get an infection. Plus, these ties are cutting into my skin."

"I told you not to fight them."

It's all I can do not to scream.

"I made roasted Brussel sprouts, beets, and chic peas."

"I said, I'm not hungry."

"I finished the blue journal." She places the tray on the bed. "You did not have a nice experience in high school. Your boyfriend back then was a real jerk. And that new girl he started dating? She was crazy."

Yeah, circle of my life.

"Please listen to me. I need up. There's a bathroom right over there. You wouldn't have put me in here if you weren't thinking I could use it. Please let me use it. I need to shower."

Nibbling the inside of her cheek, she studies me. "I guess I didn't think this through, huh?"

"Tell you what, go get the gun Quinn had. You can hold it on me the whole time. I won't cause any problems. I promise. Just get me some fresh clothes and sheets to remake this bed. *Please.*"

"You promise to be good?"

"I do."

"Do you double-triple promise?"

"I do."

She picks the tray back up, walks it from the room, then reappears with a duffel bag.

That's my duffel bag.

She places it in the bathroom.

She leaves again. Her feet tread the basement steps up and out. Several minutes later she's back with a stack of linens, a gun, and heavy-duty scissors. She puts the linens on the floor.

With the gun and heavy-duty scissors, she comes around the side of the bed. She places both of them on the mattress.

Then, she slaps me.

Stunned, I don't respond.

She yells, lunging at me, not quite touching but almost.

I flinch.

She straightens, smirking a bit.

Point proved that she's in charge I guess, she picks the gun up and points it at me. With the scissors, she cuts the plastic around my right wrist.

I remain very still.

She places the scissors next to my now free hand, and with the gun aimed, she backs up to the door. "When you're done, leave everything in a pile at the door. If I don't see the scissors right on top, I'll shoot you in the head."

Taking the key from around her neck, she closes and locks the door.

Though I can't see a camera, there's got to be one in here. She's watching. So, I take my time with the scissors, cutting first the tie on my left wrist. With a groan, I sit up and do both of my ankles. I give myself a moment to equalize before I swing my legs over the bed.

My sock-covered feet hit the floor, and carefully I stand. The room spins. I take a moment to steady myself before shuffling into the bathroom.

Shower first, then I'll change the sheets and put everything at the door just like she said. I'll be the best damn prisoner I can.

Until I figure a way out of this mess.

15

Sunday 6 a.m.

I BARELY SLEEP. Instead, I pace, do some light stretching, and eventually turn on the TV. It's pre-programmed with two channels. The first plays reruns of my favorite sitcom, *Seinfeld*. The second shows Popeye's bed upstairs in Martha's living room. I stare at that bed for hours, but Popeye never appears.

I don't like what that might mean.

When the digital clock on the TV flicks to six in the morning, the door opens. Like clockwork. I'm learning her schedule.

She stands with the gun already up and ready. "Move to the other side of the bed and stand in the corner."

I do.

With one eye on me, she rolls a serving table in with a plate and a mug on top. Leaning down, she gathers up my dirty clothes and sheets. The scissors are right on top, just like she instructed.

"Where's Popeye?" I point to the TV. "His bed has been empty all night."

"You seem to be settling in," she says instead of answering my question. "Do you like the clothes I brought over? I can get you others if you want."

"My clothes are fine. Thank you."

"I didn't do a full-on breakfast like before." Her voice softens. "I was afraid to screw it up. Instead, I made you toast with avocado. It's kind of hard to screw that up. I also made you coffee, black."

I am hungry. "Thank you."

Smiling, she nods. "Popeye is fine. No worries. I'm taking good care of him. Did you notice the bathroom had your favorite soap and shampoo?"

"Yes, thank you again."

Her face flushes. She likes pleasing me.

Martha clears her throat. "I've moved onto the green journal. You're in college now. I don't mean to be a prude, but you sure did drink a lot."

"I had my moments."

"Just so you know, that night you came over for Chinese and wine? That's the first time I've ever been drunk."

I find that hard to believe, but I jokingly reply, "Hope I'm not a bad influence."

"Oh, Jessica." She laughs. "We are meant to be the best of friends."

Whatever you've got to tell yourself, bitch.

16

S*unday 12 p.m.*

SITTING CROSS-LEGGED ON THE BED, I spread the historical romance novels out in front of me. I haven't read any of them yet. She brought them over from my house. I bought them a week ago at the local used bookstore, intending on binging one or two during my three days off.

I'm reading the back of one when the door opens. Again, like clockwork.

"Move to the back corner," Martha instructs.

I want to flip her off, but I do as she says. Anything to not be tied down again.

Holding the gun in her right hand, she steps inside my room. The serving tray from breakfast sits by the door. She double-checks everything is there, before wheeling the table out.

A few seconds later, she reappears with a cage gripped

in her left hand. Inside the cage, a hamster excitedly skitters forward to peer through the tiny bars at me.

Martha, all smiles and happiness, laughs. "I just got him. Guess what his name is?"

"I don't know."

"Guess."

I shrug. "Bandit."

"Nooo. It's Gizmo!"

"Gizmo?"

The hamster turns a circle, coming back around to peer through the tiny bars again. Martha watches it, grinning. "Don't you remember?"

"I'm not sure..."

"You had a hamster in college. You named it—"

"Gizmo."

"Yes." She laughs. "Funny thing is, I thought I knew everything about you. But I'm learning so much more by reading your journals. I've only had Gizmo for an hour, but I'm already in love. He's a sweet little thing."

Martha lifts the cage higher. The hamster comes up on its back legs. His nose twitches as he looks at her. Laughing, she mimics him.

Then once again she steps from the room, taking Gizmo with her and closing the door.

What in the hell?

17

Sunday 6 p.m.

I SPEND THE AFTERNOON READING, mostly so I won't check the TV. I can't take Popeye's bed being empty. She's playing a game with me with that camera angle. Why else torture me with my dog's empty bed?

For now, I'll trust that he's okay. I cannot give Martha the satisfaction of a response. Because she knows Popeye is my Achilles heel.

The door opens. Without her asking, I move off of the bed and over to the back corner.

It's creepy as hell when she smiles. She likes that I'm learning. Tonight, she doesn't hold the gun up and ready. It's on the serving tray that she wheels in. "From the first day that I met Quinn he talked about you. Jessica this. Jessica that. At first, I hated you. You'd so clearly screwed up this amazing man. Then, I became curious. After you accepted my friend request, I combed through your Facebook page."

I'm always so careful about requests. If I accepted hers, we must have had several friends in common—that's usually how I decide to accept or decline invitations.

"Quinn came here once from Florida. He told me he was coming for some sailing thing—a trade show or whatever. I thought, awesome, road trip! But he was adamant I not accompany him. I knew then he wanted to see you. Sure enough, I tracked his phone. He wore a disguise and went to the hospital. He sat in a chair and watched you work. You walked right past him and never knew."

My skin prickles.

"He never asked me to marry him. Oh, I hinted. But he never did. You were his one and only. You're lucky I'm not a jealous woman."

An unexpected laugh escapes me. I cough to hide it.

"Anyway, I'm almost done with the pink journal. You're in your senior year of college. That means you're about to meet Quinn." A long pause follows. Her gaze moves off of me, to the empty TV screen, down to the food, over to the novels on the bed, before once again looking at me. "Do you ever think you'd marry again?"

"No." My time with Quinn did me in.

"I've never tied the knot. I would. He'd have to be special—definitely someone who has never been married before. I've learned my lesson there. Also, no kids. Talk about baggage. Though, I wouldn't mind one of my own."

She sighs, looking again at the black TV screen with the intermittent day and time flicking on. "Have you been watching Popeye?"

She knows I haven't.

"Eggplant, Portobello mushroom, spinach lasagna." Martha nods to the tray.

Quinn's favorite.

"Our Quinn's favorite," she says, taking the key from around her neck and stepping from the room.

Now he's *our* Quinn?

18

Sunday 9 p.m.

I'M in bed reading when the door opens. *Not* like clockwork. I'm so shocked to see Martha off schedule that I don't move.

Jaw clenched tight, she glares at me. "You're a bitch."

"Excuse me?"

"First, you have a one-night stand with Quinn. Then you don't return his calls. Then you hook up with someone else?"

"Martha, it was college."

"YOU TREATED HIM LIKE SHIT."

Her outburst stuns me. I freeze.

"Why?"

"*Why?*"

"Yes. WHY?" Martha stomps over to the tray where I placed my dirty dishes. She grabs the thick plastic plate and hurls it at me. My arms come up, but the plate connects with the brick wall behind me to bounce off and land on the bed.

With a scream, she grabs the dirty spork and throws it at me. Like the plate, it connects with the brick wall and bounces to the bed.

Fists clenched, she glares at me. "I thought you were some mysterious woman that I could learn from. You'd teach me what I did wrong with Quinn. But I was mistaken. To think I wasted so much time on you. I don't want to learn a single thing from you. I'm done. You can rot in here. No more homemade meals. No more me checking on you either."

From the back of her waistband, she pulls out the gun. She points it at me. "Die, for all I care."

She shoots.

I scream.

19

Sunday 9:15 p.m.

Blood oozes from my left thigh. For a moment, I don't move. I stay very still. Like I'm afraid if I do move, Martha will come back in.

But I hear only the sound of the running toilet in my bathroom.

After another few beats, I take in a deep breath. Fire licks across my leg. I force myself to get up. The muscles in my left thigh pulse as I slide that leg across the mattress. Pain like I've never felt contracts through every nerve and fiber—from my toes up to my hips. With a hiss, I stop moving. My body sags back against the pillows. I suck in a breath and then blow it out hard.

Okay, Jessica, you can do this.

I can either fling myself out of this bed like ripping a Band-Aid, or I can slow-and-steady-wins-the-race.

I opt for the latter.

Using my right arm and leg for momentum, I roll, landing on my stomach first and then sliding to the floor. My good leg touches down. I put all my weight on it as I hold onto the edge of the bed. The room spins. I squeeze my eyes shut. My fingers dig into the mattress. I breathe.

When I feel more centered, I open my eyes. My gaze lands on the bloody mattress with a singed hole, which means that's hopefully where the bullet is and not in my thigh.

Quickly, I check, burrowing into the singed area with my index finger. Sure enough, I bring out the bullet. Thank God.

Now to see how bad it is.

Putting all my weight on the mattress, I hop on my good leg. Pain rockets through my left thigh. I grit my teeth, and I hop again. One more hop and I'm to the end of the bed.

I allow myself a second or two to once again breathe. I need something to hold onto, but between here and the bathroom stretches five feet of open space. I'm just going to do it, and if I crash, I crash.

It's the only option.

I hop.

I breathe.

I hop again.

I wince.

One more, and I wobble.

My arms come out, floundering for anything to hold onto. But I lose my balance and crash to the floor, right on top of my bad leg.

I cry out. Excruciating pain clenches my thigh. Nausea rolls through my stomach and straight into my throat. I dry heave.

There's no way I'm getting up and off this floor.

Slowly, I crawl, pulling myself toward the bathroom. Through the door, I go, over to the toilet. I pray I don't yank it off the wall as I wrench myself up to sit. Above the toilet is a cabinet fastened to the wall with a rudimentary first aid kit inside. I fling the cabinet door open. The momentum sends several items crashing down—extra soap, tampons, shampoo, toothpaste, and the kit.

The bathroom spins. I close my eyes. I inhale. I exhale.

I have nothing to cut my leggings with. Instead, I wedge my fingers into the hole already created by the bullet. Gently, I tear away the cotton fabric and work it down my leg. The gray material parts easily, allowing me to view things.

The bullet went through my outer left thigh, missing bone and artery. Small blessings. The inner thigh would have left me dead, most likely. There's an entry and exit wound. I take a towel and apply pressure to control the bleeding. I'll need a few stitches, but for now, I'll hold it closed with tape from the first aid kit.

About an inch in diameter, the bullet parted my thigh creating a floral pattern with flaps of folded skin. Red bruising radiates out in all directions. That'll be blue by tomorrow.

Cleaning this is going to hurt like hell.

I maneuver myself over onto the tub and get my bad leg inside. I turn the water on to a tepid temperature. Using my hands, I cup a generous amount and glide it over the wound.

A hiss escapes my gritted teeth. The first one is always the worst.

I repeat, cupping water and flowing it over the area—both entry and exit. I eye the wound carefully for metal fragments, but I see exactly what I should be—fresh meat, blood, and skin. Next, comes mild soap that I gently use and rinse—hissing and gritting my teeth the entire time. After that, I allow my leg to air dry.

From the first aid kit, I take the tape and tear off several thin sections to close the wound, both entry, and exit. I wrap my entire thigh—front to back—in gauze. I need antibiotics and proper stitches.

When Martha comes back, I'll beg her for some.

If she comes back.

She has to.

She wouldn't leave me in here to die. Would she?

20

Monday 6 a.m.

"I take it this cutie belongs to you?"

"You're not going to believe this, but I'm also a nurse."

"Want to come over later?"

"It's like a haunted house. You can come in, but you're not leaving."

"A secure bunker for when the Zombie Apocalypse happens."

Martha's voice comes distorted, kicking up speed, overlapping.

"The thought of a friend coming over motivated me."

"By the way, malbec is my favorite."

"It has been so long since I hung out with a girlfriend."

"If there's a hot tub and martini at the bottom I'm in."

"I think we're each other's doppelgänger."

Her blurry face floats across my brain, surging in and then recoiling away.

When next I hear her voice it's clear and close. "Wakey-wakey."

My eyes tug open. Martha stands in the open door, staring at me lying on the bed. I've got my bad leg propped up on a pillow. From her spot yards away, she studies the bandage. I note she's already wheeled in my breakfast.

"And to think I wasn't aiming. Hm." She wears a light-weight blue plaid flannel that I recognize from my closest. She's also holding the plastic plate and spork that she threw. Which means she came over to my bed while I was sleeping and retrieved them from where I left them on the mattress.

There's a brightness to her eyes that hasn't been there before. It's like she didn't even shoot me and leave me in here to die.

She's holding something behind her back. "I had a great idea." She shows me a box of hair dye and a pair of scissors. "Thought we'd do your hair today." She swishes hers back and forth. "This used to be your style."

"I don't want to do my hair." I motion to my leg. "In case you haven't noticed, I've been shot. I need antibiotics and proper stitches."

She once again looks at my leg. "How bad does it hurt?"

"Horribly bad."

"Tell you what, eat breakfast and then do your hair. I'll go get the things you need. Deal?"

Do I have a choice? "Deal."

21

Monday 12 p.m.

WITH ALL MY weight on my good leg, I stand in the bathroom and cut my long brown hair up to my chin. It comes off in uneven chunks that I toss into the toilet. I have no emotional connection to my hair. Never have. Long, medium, short, pixy—I've done it all. It's just hair. It'll grow.

Still, I'd managed to grow it quite a bit. I'm sad to see nearly a foot of it flush into the sewer.

Next, I open the box of black dye, quickly mix, and work it through my newly short hair. I've colored at home multiple times. I don't need to read the directions.

While it sets, I eat the breakfast she brought—a toasted bagel with peanut butter and black coffee. I place the tray by the door, making sure the hair scissors are right on top and visible.

When thirty minutes expires, I wash and rinse the dye

out in the sink. It's easier than maneuvering my whole body and bad leg into the tub.

On the dot, the door opens at noon.

Martha gasps. "We're twinsies!"

She has nothing that I requested—no antibiotics or a suture kit. Instead, she holds the pink journal—the one that caused her to shoot me.

She grins. "I had another great idea."

"We had a deal. Where are the antibiotics and the suture kit?"

She waves that off. "You'll be fine." She holds up the pink journal. "When I was a little girl, my father would make me rip up school work that wasn't good enough. Or he'd burn bad drawings. Sometimes he'd shred things. And a few times he made me eat particularly sub-par items."

"Eat?"

"It was his way of showing me how to wipe clean and start over until things were done right."

She tosses the journal. It lands on the corner of the bed farthest away. I eye it.

"Now obviously I don't want you to eat the entire journal. But I want you to rip out the pages where you first meet Quinn. No longer will there be a one-night stand. Or you not returning his calls. And definitely not you hooking up with someone else. We're going to erase the past."

"You want me to eat the pages of that journal?"

"Yes."

"You've got to be kidding me."

"You've never done anything like this before, but you'll see. It's for the best."

"Eating those pages is not going to erase the past."

Martha watches me. Quietly she says, "Eat the pages, Jessica."

My gaze drops to the journal. I can't do this. One page, okay. But if memory serves me, the entire last half of the journal is about my first few months with Quinn. Generally, it is safe to eat paper, but I don't want to put that to a test. It'll cause a stomach ache, for sure, and probably a bowel blockage.

"Jessica."

"I'm more than willing to rip out every page and tear them up. Or burn them. Or shred them. But eating them will make me violently ill, Martha."

"Nah, you'll probably get sick. But not violently ill. Don't exaggerate. I've eaten enough paper to know." She nods to the journal.

I don't move.

With a sigh, she brings the gun out from where she tucked it into the back of her waistband. She points it at me. "I was hoping we'd moved past the gun thing."

I am not winning this, and I don't doubt for a second that she will shoot me again.

With a deep breath, I push up to my elbow. My jaw clamps tight as I stretch over and snag the journal. An involuntary groan pushes up my throat. My body flops back into place. A wave of nausea bitters my mouth. I cringe.

"Boy, you are in pain, huh?"

Bitch.

I open the journal and flip pages. I find the first entry with Quinn's name and I rip it from the seam. Thankfully, the pages of this particular journal are made of recycled paper and on the normal side. My earlier journals are comprised of parchment. There's no way to eat that.

I continue ripping pages as Martha watches. Twenty in all. I close the journal and toss it back. It lands at her feet.

"It's for your own good," she says.

Robotically, I tear off a chunk of the first page and I cram it in my mouth. On the bedside table sits a bottle of water. I take a sip. I swallow. I tear off the next piece, chew, swallow. The next. Chew. Swallow. I keep going, staring at Martha the entire time.

"Gosh, I wasn't allowed to chase it with water. Does that help?"

I don't answer that stupid question.

I tear, chew, and swallow.

Tear, chew, swallow.

Tear, chew, swallow.

In a daze, I continue until all twenty pieces of journal paper are in my stomach.

Martha watches me in amazement.

When I swallow the last piece, she smiles. "I've never witnessed that from this end of things. Interesting."

I can't take my eyes off of her. I hate her.

Leaning down, she picks up the journal that I tossed.

The doorbell rings.

The sound comes so loud and shockingly clear, that I freeze.

Then, I scream, "Help!"

Martha laughs. "We can hear them, but they can't hear us. Go ahead, scream. Help!" she imitates me. "Help!"

I cry.

She moves away to look at the monitor on the other side of the basement. I wish I could see it from here. She comes back. "Looks like it's Girl Scout cookie time. They'll go away."

The doorbell rings again.

"Help," I sob. "*Help.*"

"Oh." Her bottom lip pokes out. "Don't be like that. It's not so bad down here. You've got a crate of snacks that you haven't even touched, two homemade and hand-delivered meals per day, a private bathroom, books, and a TV you never watch.

She glances over her shoulder at the monitor. "Yep, they're already heading off. Probably going in the direction of your house. They're going to strike out on this street. Poor little things."

Martha steps from the room. "I was thinking tonight I'd make pasta with garlic and olive oil. It'll help things slide through. Sound good?"

I glare.

With that, she takes the key from around her neck, closes the door, and locks it.

Slowly, I make my way into the bathroom. I stick my finger down my throat and throw up.

22

Monday 6 p.m.

MARTHA SITS on a chair in the open door, watching rerun episodes of *Seinfeld* on the wall-mounted TV. In front of her sits a foldable table with the gun and an empty plate that was full of pasta swimming in olive oil.

She laughs. "I see why you like this show so much."

My plate, still full, sits on a tray that she placed on top of the mattress.

Behind her, something flickers. I can't see the monitor on the other side of the basement, but if I sit up, I should be able to.

I do, with great effort, pretending to straighten my sock. Martha spares me a glance, before going back to the TV. I look beyond her, sure enough seeing the large screen. But from this angle, I can't make anything out.

Abruptly, she stands.

I finish with my sock and lie back down.

"See, two best friends hanging out watching TV and eating dinner. Isn't this great?" With one eye on me, she slides her foldable table from the room. "Thought you'd like to know that Popeye and Gizmo are best friends. Doesn't that make you happy? You never ask about him."

Just hearing Popeye's name makes my heart skip a happy beat. "When can I see him?"

"Mm, I'll let you know." Still, with one eye on me, she leans down and picks up a paper bag sitting just outside the door. "I have a surprise for you." She tosses it toward me. It lands right on top of my uneaten pasta in olive oil. "Oh, now look. You've made a mess."

No, *you* made the mess.

Gingerly, I pick it up, holding it between my thumb and middle finger. A dark oily spot spreads along the paper bag. "What is it?"

"Open it."

From the bag, I take out a new pink journal.

"Now that you purged your past, I want you to rewrite it. You've got a shield around your heart that needs cracking. I want you to meet Quinn all over again. Detail everything you would do differently now that you're older and wiser."

"Excuse me?"

"You didn't mean to, but you hurt him."

"You do understand it is in the past? Nothing changes just because I rewrite those first months with him."

She walks over to the TV and pushes the channel button, putting it on Popeye's bed channel. As usual, it's empty. But it works, I'll do what she wants.

She nods to the journal. "You'll also find a pen in there."

I stare at her.

"Know that journal wasn't exactly cheap," she says primly. "The leather binding alone racked up the price."

Idly, I run my hands along the embossed cover with spiral seaming. As I do, an idea forms. "It's a pretty pink. I would love to be able to wear this color, but unfortunately, I can't. You however would look great in this color."

A flush creeps into her cheeks. "Oh." She covers her face with her hands. "Don't be silly."

"I'm serious."

"You really think?" She peers at me between her fingers.

"I do."

We share a smile.

"I love it," I say. "The only thing is..."

"What?"

"Well, the original journal was this color."

Her hands slide from her face. "That's why I got that one."

"Yes, and that makes sense. But if I'm going to rewrite the past, shouldn't it be a whole new journal? Fresh start, right?"

Her smile fades.

"Maybe a yellow one? Or white? Or even black. Just as long as it's a new color."

"I don't think they had any other colors."

"Sure they did. It's no big deal. You kept the receipt, right? Just take this one back and return it for a new one."

"I can't take that one back. It's greasy."

"Oh." I wince. "It is, isn't it? And here I was already brainstorming my new Quinn pages." I sigh, heavy and deep. "I was even hoping to run a few ideas by you."

"You were?"

I place the journal aside. "If only I had a new color..."

"Fine." She throws her hands up.

"If you could also get me some antibiotics. I wasn't sure

if you remembered. There are some at my house if you don't have any."

"Anything else?" The features of her face pinch.

I keep a pleasant voice. "No, thank you."

Her eyes narrow.

My brows go up. "What's wrong, Martha?"

"I'll tell you what's wrong. This whole room is for you. I made sure it was stocked with your favorite snacks, bathroom items, clothes, books, a TV with your favorite show, and all you've done is complain." Her voice lifts in mimicry. "My leg hurts. I don't eat meat. I'm wearing a diaper. I want to see Popeye. I don't like mayonnaise. It's the wrong color journal!"

She charges over and flips the tray of uneaten oily noodles. They upend on my lap. Before I register what she's done, she whirls away and stomps from the room.

The door slams. It locks.

I laugh as I pick up the plastic spork covered in noodles. This would be a good weapon, but unfortunately, she'll notice if it's gone. I put it back down.

Next, I take the pen from the journal and give it a study. I think this will work for what I have in mind. I climb from the bed.

Now, let's see if I still got it.

23

Monday 6:30 p.m.

WHEN I WAS A KID, I got locked out of our house. I used the clip from a pen and a paper clip to break in.

I don't have a paper clip, but I do have the wire binding of this journal.

It's thick and takes me a few seconds to work an area free, straighten, and then bend it into a ninety-degree angle. I quickly re-do the binding so Martha doesn't realize I took a section.

Next, I take the clip from the pen.

I don't bother cleaning the mess she made when she threw my food on me. Instead, I drip noodles as I limp from the bed and across the room.

Halfway there, I pause, breathing through the brutal pain blasting in my thigh. The next few steps come strained, but I make it to the door.

I bend down, forcing myself to ignore the pain, and I insert the binding wire into the bottom of the lock. I put tension on it at a downward angle, hoping it's strong enough. It seems to be. Next, I poke the pen's clip into the top of the lock. I push until it stops. I scrub it up and down, feeling for the catch of the interior workings. As I do, I rotate the wire counterclockwise, praying it releases.

After half a dozen tries, nothing happens. When I did this as a kid, it worked so quickly. I worry the binding wire isn't strong enough for the tension.

With all my weight on my good leg, I straighten up. *I can do this.* I'm just about to try again when the pen's clip slides from the lock to clink onto the floor.

Well, shit.

Holding onto the wall, I keep my left leg up and bend forward. Thank God I do yoga. But the pain gets me. I involuntarily cry out right as my fingers grasp the clip, and clutching it tightly, I right myself.

I try again with the lock, scrubbing the clip up and down in the narrow keyhole. But it doesn't work.

A frustrated breath growls from me. "Come on, Jessica. You did this as a kid. You can do this again."

I try a new angle with the tension of the binding wire. It clicks. It rotates.

You'd think I'd just conquered Mount Kilimanjaro with the relief that hits me.

The door cracks open. I heave a sigh.

I hop from my prison out into the other area of the basement. It smells musty. I spy the step ladder propped against the wall. It only comes to my hips, but I use it as a makeshift crutch. Every inch comes with great effort as I work my way over to the large screen monitor. Sweat gathers in my cleavage and along my hairline. I feel pale. I hope I don't pass out.

My gaze flits across the multiple images. I spy Popeye in the living room, curled in his bed. Tears pop into my eyes. He looks unharmed and very content.

That's the same view I have on my TV but he's not on it. She's showing me a fake video.

Bitch.

The rest of the house sits empty. She's gone to get me my new journal.

The split screen in the upper left corner shows my room. I knew she was watching. From the angle, I can tell the camera is hidden in the upper right corner with only a tiny view of my bathroom. Good to know. I study all the camera views. This side of the basement appears to be the only area not filmed.

The camera that covers the porch still looks over onto the Airbnb. There is no car there, but still, I press the "Talk" button.

"Hello? Is anyone there?" I wait. "Hello?"

Nothing.

If I ever get out of here, I swear I am moving into the busiest neighborhood I can find.

No, not if. *When* I get out of here.

Turning away from the monitor, I eye the steps up to the door out of this place. At the landing, everything has been repaired where I hammered my way into the drywall to expose the phone line. I'm sure that amused Martha to no end.

She's probably changed the code, but here goes nothing.

Using the makeshift crutch, I hobble over. There is no banister to use as support. So, I sit down on the third step.

Slowly, I crab crawl my way up to the top and pull myself to stand.

0-8-0-5-7-0

It doesn't work.

I don't try again because I don't want to time the system out. She'll know I've been roaming.

From up here, I look around. When I opened my prison door, a section of the shelves swung outward. I have to admit, the hidden door is clever.

The shelves remain stuffed with the same supplies including a few new things like my journals, more historical romance novels, and piles of folded clothes taken from my closet.

In the corner is the oversized beanbag that was there before, but now there's an opened bag of popcorn and a can of soda. She probably lounges there, munching away, watching me on the monitor.

Creepy damn woman.

Slowly, I descend the steps, once again crab-walking my way down. At the bottom, I use my makeshift crutch to assist me over to the shelves. The large first aid kit that was there before sits centered on the bottom one. I open it and rifle through, selecting a suture kit and more gauze. Unfortunately, there are no antibiotics.

I close it and push it back into place, making sure it's exactly where it was.

On the top shelf is the midsized green and white toolbox —it's my best bet for a weapon. Clicking open the stepladder, I position it in place. It takes me way too long to climb the two steps. But eventually, I balance in place.

Any other day I would effortlessly pick this toolbox up, but I can't risk losing my already precarious stability. Instead, I maneuver it to the edge. Reaching up and over, I grasp the handle with my right hand and hold on to the shelf with my left, all while putting weight onto my good leg.

The movement is awkward. Something shifts inside the box, redirecting the weight. The tools slide. My body tilts. I recognize I'm losing balance, but I don't care. I want this damn thing. My left hand loses hold of the shelf. My right hand releases the handle. I topple backward off the two-step ladder. My left foot catches in the rung, and I land hard on my butt. I cry out. I just tore open the wound.

I don't move. Instead, I stare up at the toolbox balanced on the shelf's ledge like one tiny breath will make it come down right on top of me. From down here on my butt, it looks so far away.

Slowly, so as not to disturb the gentle balancing act the tools are in, I inch my left leg free from the ladder. Inch by inch, I get back on my good leg. Blood seeps through the gauze, but I ignore it and the pain as I once again awkwardly ascend the two tiny steps of the ladder.

Sweat trails the side of my face. I breathe through the faintness I feel coming on. With my right hand, I once again grasp the handle and this time manage to get it from the top shelf down to the middle one and eye level with me.

A tiny lock secures the clasp.

No.

This wasn't here before.

I yank it. It doesn't move. You've got to be kidding me.

My head drops. I blow out an angry breath. All that work—

Wait a minute. My head lifts. My heart surges. It's one of those toolboxes with a shallow top tray where people usually put surplus screws or whatever. I open it, hoping beyond all hopes...loudly, I laugh.

Wild excitement dances through me. *Yes.* There's a small plastic box cutter.

An acute awareness crawls my skin. I glance over at the monitor. Martha pulls into the driveway.

Quickly, I stash the plastic item in my bra and snap the lid on the tray. I get the toolbox back up onto the top shelf. I have to come to the tip of my right toes to fully position it exactly as it was before.

On the monitor, Martha opens her car door.

More blood oozes through the gauze. I make a calculated move, jumping the two steps and landing hard on my good leg. It jars my bad one. I wince.

I get the ladder snapped back together and hop-hobble it to where I found it leaning up against the wall.

Martha's now at the front door.

The ladder falls. I scramble to pick it up and reposition it.

Martha steps into the house.

I teeter into my room. I'm about to close the door. My gaze sweeps the basement, making sure everything looks as it did.

No! I left the suture kit and gauze on the bottom shelf next to the first aid kit. *Shit.*

Martha walks into the living room to pet Popeye.

I move fast, using both my legs, biting down hard to keep from crying out. I make it over to the bottom shelf and grab the items.

Martha walks swiftly toward the kitchen.

I lunge, dragging my left leg behind me. My hands reach out. I bite down against the pain. My fingers dig into the hidden door frame. I don't chance another look at the monitor as I shut myself in. The pen's clip and binding wire hang from the lock. I attack them, jiggling things back into place.

I dive toward the bed. My hand shoves under the mattress, stashing the lock pick materials, suture kit, and gauze. I try to get up, but I slip on the oily noodles and land hard on the floor. I cry out, fighting to move, but the pain is unreal. Instead, I lie back on the concrete and I don't move. I'm about to throw up.

A minute ticks by.

The lock clicks.

Panting and soaked with sweat, I look up at Martha.

Between the mess of noodles and my bloody leg, it looks bad.

A strange look crosses her face that I think is more concern than suspicion. "Are you okay?"

"No, I'm not okay!" I explode, waving at my leg. "I told you I need antibiotics, proper stitching, and goddammit, I need pain pills. This thing hurts like hell!"

Her head cocks. Tenderly, she looks at me. She reaches inside the pocket of the hoodie she's wearing and brings out a prescription bottle of pills. She throws it at me, then turns and steps out of the room.

I read the bottle. Antibiotics. Thank God.

She reappears, holding up the first aid kit I already rifled through. She opens it. "What do you need?"

"Suture kit and gauze." Thankfully, there were multiples of everything. She won't realize I've already been in it.

It takes her a second to find the items, then she tosses them to me along with Tylenol. "I'm going to need that suture kit back once you're done using it."

I crawl over to the bathroom, carrying the items with me. The box cutter down inside my bra pokes me, reminding me I now have a weapon. Just the thought brings me comfort.

Carefully, she follows me. She stays at a distance as I balance on the tub, unwrap my leg, clean it and suture it. I don't know if it's the all-around pain I'm in, but I barely feel the stitching as I do it.

"I've been doing a bit of soul-searching. I never really had a friend before." She fiddles with her fingers. "I think it's because I'm hard to get along with. I don't want to be hard to get along with, but somehow I am. I wish I would have had what you and Quinn had. Hopefully one day I will."

It's everything I can do not to roll my eyes. "I had to file a restraining order against him. Did you know that?"

"I did." Her voice lights up. "I would have loved for Quinn to be that obsessed with me."

I have no response. I simply keep closing my wound up. Quietly, she watches.

"Well anyway, I found a new journal. I'll leave it on the bed. It's silver. I'm excited to see what you come up with. Maybe you can start tomorrow morning after you rest and heal. You should also probably clean your room."

"Fine."

She hesitates. "Are you mad at me?"

I summon every bit of patience. "I'm frustrated."

"At me?"

"At this whole situation. I'm not meant to be locked up down here. What do you think I'm going to do if you let me go? Do you think I'm going to tell on you? Do you think you're going to get in trouble? Honestly, I just want Popeye and I want to go home. I won't tell anybody anything."

She thinks about my words so long that I go back to stitching up my leg. Eventually, I'm done and I wrap it with fresh gauze. I take two of the antibiotics plus Tylenol. When

I look up at her, she's still standing outside the bathroom door looking at me. I don't see the gun. She's probably got it tucked down inside the back of her waistband. I could lunge and attack, but I'm too weak.

For a brief second, I think she might just let me go.

"But if I release you, you'll no longer be my friend." She turns, and I do see the gun in her leggings. I was right.

Taking the plate, the spork, the greasy pink journal, and the suture kit, she leaves. She never even looks at the pen and its missing clip.

24

Tuesday 6 a.m.

Now that I know where the camera is, I'm careful with my movements. Though I stashed multiple things under the mattress, I don't retrieve them. Not yet. Martha is not to be underestimated, and I need my strength to battle her.

With the noodle mess cleaned, fresh sheets once again on the bed, and me in clean clothes, I lounge against the pillows as I idly watch *Seinfeld* on TV. Beside me on the nightstand is the new silver journal with the pen inside.

The door opens. Martha appears with breakfast. "Now that you've had a good night's rest and will soon have food in your belly, I expect to see pages written in your journal."

Carefully, she approaches the bed, and with her eyes on me the entire time, she slides the tray onto the edge. Then quickly, she backs away. I stay very still, letting her know I'm not a threat. Her comfort level equals letting her guard down. And that is when I'll make my move.

At the door, she picks up the pile of dirty sheets and walks out. Using the key around her neck, she locks the door.

I note she doesn't have the gun tucked into the back of her pajama bottoms. It's the first time she's come in here without that weapon.

This morning she made me oatmeal with walnuts and banana. With the spork I eat it all, chasing it with the black coffee she always brings me. I take an antibiotic and two Tylenol. I am feeling better.

Done with breakfast, I limp the tray over to the door. Then I make my way into the bathroom. The camera mounted in the top right corner of my cell gives a view of the entire room with just a sliver of the sink in the bathroom. The toilet and tub are out of shot.

Now that I have that knowledge, I sit on the tub and take the small plastic box cutter from my bra. Briefly, I looked at this last night, but I was in too much pain to study it. Now though, I slide the lever up, eyeing the tiny blade. It's one of those retractable razors with multiple snapping points. This one's been used a lot. There's only one edge left in the dispenser. I test it with my finger. Unfortunately, it's not too sturdy. One hard jab and the blade will break off.

Still, I have this. I simply need to figure out how to make it into a viable weapon.

25

Tuesday 12 p.m.

I HAVEN'T WRITTEN any words.

I'm not a writer. I don't know what she expects. I journal my thoughts, just like a million other people. I don't know how to make stuff up. And that's what she wants—a story about Quinn that is all hearts and flowers.

The truth is, I met him at a frat party and slept with him. I wasn't drunk, but I was buzzed. After, I ignored his calls. When I saw him on campus, I would turn and go the other way. I don't know what my problem was. Maybe I liked him more than I wanted to admit. It wasn't that I was embarrassed about the one-night stand. It's just that I was in college. I *wanted* to party and sleep around. I figured long-term stuff would come later.

But he wouldn't leave me alone. He showed up everywhere with over-the-top gestures like singing grams, buckets of flowers, hell, he even washed and waxed my car. Looking back, I should have seen the signs of what became an obsessed and controlling man, but I gradually softened. I'd never had a boy be so persistently sweet to me.

Our one-night stand turned into an actual date. That turned into another which eventually became a relationship. We were engaged by graduation and married soon after. Truthfully, we were happy.

Until we weren't.

I caught him looking through my things. Following me. Showing up to my work. Accusing a male co-worker of being in love with me. Confronting my friends that they were too involved in our lives. Making me pick between him and my friends. He even forbid me to take my birth control pills. He demanded I get pregnant.

Then the worst night of my life happened when he forced himself on me.

I finally woke the hell up, faced my inner coward, and realized I needed to leave. I thought I had effectively turned that page in my life.

How naïve and stupid of me.

And now he's dead.

DEAD. DEAD. DEAD.

These are the words I carve into the first page of the silver journal. Nothing else, just DEAD.

I rip that page out and ball it up. How am I supposed to make up fluff about a man I grew to hate?

As expected, the door opens. Martha doesn't look at me as she walks over to the wall-mounted TV and turns it on. She presses the channel button to Popeye's empty bed.

It does not have the effect she wants.

She walks right back out.

With a deep breath, I look over at the stack of historical romance novels. An idea hits me. I thumb through the one sitting on top of the stack, find where the hero and heroine meet, and begin to write.

26

Tuesday 6 p.m.

SOMEWHERE DURING THE AFTERNOON, I doze off. When I awake, Martha stands beside my bed holding the silver journal and reading what I wrote. When she notices I'm awake, she takes a big step back.

Still not trusting me.

Clearing my throat, I sit up.

She flips a page and keeps on reading.

"Can I go to the bathroom?"

With another big step away from the bed, she nods.

Carefully, I slide to my feet. I put pressure on my left leg, pleased to see it's better. I don't let her know that, though, as I limp to the bathroom and do my thing.

Minutes later, I come out to find her still reading. I didn't write that much. She's either a slow reader or is combing through my words a second time. I stay where I am, hovering at the bathroom door.

"This is stupid." Loudly, she closes the journal. "It's clear you copied this from one of your historical romance novels. You simply changed the names and put them in a current time period."

This is true.

On second thought, she opens the journal back up and rips the pages out.

"I'm not eating those," I say.

She tears the pages into chunks and surprises the hell out of me when she shoves them into her mouth. Stunned, I watch.

Defiantly, she stares at me—chewing, swallowing—as if she's trying to prove a point.

What point? That she can eat paper?

When she's done, she tosses the journal onto the bed. "Try again. This time don't copy someone else's work. That's plagiarism."

Just outside the door sits the table she usually rolls in with my food. She's not feeding me tonight. I didn't please her.

Shooting me an angry look, she exits the room, locking me in.

I hobble over to the crate of snacks and choose a Larabar. Guess this is dinner tonight.

As I munch on it, I lie back on the bed and stare at the ceiling. I'm sure she's out there reclining in her beanbag, watching me.

I had a beanbag in high school. It was checkered purple. I used to curl sideways in it and watch old movies from my father's VCR collection. There's this one I watched a few times mainly because Dad once told me it was Mom's favorite movie—*Bringing Up Baby.*

It's about a scientist who is trying to get a big grant from a society matron. Enter his love interest (the matron's niece) who immediately falls for the scientist and chaos ensues.

I can use that plot and rewrite it to make it me and Quinn.

More excited than I should be about this, I pick up the pen.

I'm three pages in when the door opens again. Martha wheels my dinner in. "See? You look happy. I knew you would be."

In my mind, I flip her off.

27

Wednesday 6 a.m.

I'M in the bathroom when the door opens. I hear Martha take out last night's meal and bring in breakfast. She shuffles close to my bed, then away. I take my time washing my face, brushing my teeth, and changing my bandage. When I emerge, she stands over in the doorway eagerly reading.

She wheeled my morning food over to the bed. I sit on the edge and eat toast with almond butter and cut pineapple. Then I sip the black coffee and watch as she flips a page and keeps reading. She makes no sound and her face holds no expression. It takes her forever. I don't know what she's thinking, but if she doesn't like it, I'm out of ideas.

With coffee done, I pick up the novel I was reading and open where I last left off.

Minutes tick by.

In my peripheral I see a small smile curve her lips. I

must have done something to make her happy. She turns back to the beginning and reads everything again.

It's going to be a while.

Like a child, she giggles as she finally closes the journal and holds it to her chest. "Oh, Jessica. You did good." Happily, she dances in place. "I love how Quinn is such a gentleman. I love how he needs money for school and he's up for a big scholarship by some hoity-toity old lady. I love that you're the old lady's granddaughter. I love that you met on a golf course when you tried to play his ball. I love how free-spirited you are, and scatterbrained. I love that you have a mean dog and Quinn's the only one who can calm him. I love how the dog hides Quinn's things to keep him around. I love that Quinn had to wear your skimpy robe because your dog stashed his clothes in the cushions of the couch. I love how Quinn takes the fall for something you did and he ends up in jail—only to be bailed out by you. I love..."

That's a lot of love.

"...how you profess your feelings, but he walks away. I love how he doesn't want to take advantage of you, given who your grandmother is."

Yep, pretty much the plot to *Bringing Up Baby*—more or less.

"I love how he has dark curly hair again. I miss that hair. I didn't like it when he shaved it." She squeezes the journal to her chest even tighter. "What comes next?"

"Excuse me?"

"What comes next?"

"Nothing, that's it. The end."

Her grin slides. "No, that can't be it. You have to end up together."

"Okay, then we end up together."

Her face falls even more. "But I need the details."

I close the novel I'm reading. "He ends up getting the scholarship by no connection to me. My grandmother picks him over a hundred other applicants. Um...she dies, and I inherit a ton of money. We live happily ever after."

"But how do you get back together?"

"It's years later. He graduates from college and becomes a research scientist. I have all this money and am looking for things to donate to. I donate to his research fund, not realizing he's connected. I'm touring his lab when we meet again. He admits that he's loved me all along and that our time in college was the best of his life. We live happily ever after. The end."

Biting the inside of her cheek, she thinks about that. "Okay, that might work. I wish you would've written a love scene, though."

The toast becomes a dead weight in my gut. The thought of writing me and Quinn making love physically makes me ill.

She places the journal on the far corner of the bed, touching it gently as if it is gold. She starts to leave.

"Wait."

She turns back. "Yes?"

"Let's have dinner tonight. Like we did before. We watched *Seinfeld* and ate noodles." Or rather she ate the noodles and then threw mine on me.

"Really?"

"Really. You can even sit way over there by the door." I shrug. "I'd love the company. It gets lonely in here."

"Okay, it's a date!" Still grinning, she backs out of the room, closing and locking the door.

I once again make my way into the bathroom. From my

bra, I take out the box cutter. I remove the thin breakable blade and set it aside. Using the brick wall, I begin shaping the small plastic item into something I never in my life thought I would make.

A shiv.

28

W*ednesday 6 p.m.*

"When I was younger my grandmother and I used to have slumber parties." I sip the malbec Martha poured me. "We'd make popcorn and mix in M&M's with loads of butter and salt. We'd find a fun movie to watch." I place the wine glass on the table beside my bed. It's the first time she's given me a real glass to drink from. That along with an actual plate and metal utensils encourages me. "Maybe we can do that sometime. Heck, we even painted each other's nails and did facials."

From over near the door, Martha smiles. "That sounds fun."

Jokingly, I say, "Of course, you'll have to move away from that door. We can't very well paint each other's nails from feet away." I fork off a bite of vegetable lasagna and eat it. "You did a great job with this."

"Thank you." She eats a piece of garlic bread. "I use fresh herbs, never dry. That's what makes any dish."

"Well, it is excellent. Better than any restaurant." I eat another bite. *Seinfeld* plays softly in the background. "You look nice tonight," I say. "Are you wearing makeup?"

She shrugs. "Just a little."

"It's pretty."

A flush crawls her neck. A few seconds go by. We eat in awkward silence.

"How about a toast?"

"Okay." She lifts her wine glass.

"To friendship." I toast the air.

"To friendship," she echoes.

We sip.

"Martha, will you tell me about yourself? Your *real* self, not the made-up version. You know everything about me, and I know nothing about you except that you were Quinn's lover."

Just the word "lover" makes me want to gag.

"Where should I start?"

"Childhood. You know I grew up in Florida with a retired Marine who drove a semi-truck. You know my mother left when I was a little girl. My grandmother pitched in where she could. How about your parents?" I point my finger at her. "The truth."

"I'm an only child to older parents." She places her wine glass on her TV table. "Mom had me when she was forty-eight. Dad was sixty."

"Wow."

"They were indifferent to my existence."

"Was it true about eating paper?"

"Yes, that's the only interaction I had with my father."

"I'm sorry."

She shrugs. "They died in an accident when I was seventeen." She wipes her fingers with a cloth napkin. "I inherited *a lot* of money."

"Oh, yeah?"

"Yeah, more than you can imagine."

She's lied her fool head off so many times, I'm not sure what to believe. But a certain note to her tone tells me this is her truth. "Did you go to college?"

"I had a nanny, a maid, a driver, a whole wing of a house for my bedroom. I went to the best boarding schools. I was constantly in trouble. I was the cliché rich kid. I went to exactly one semester of university and dropped out."

"What did you do?"

"I lived off my trust fund and I traveled." She tears off a bite of garlic bread and swipes it through tomato sauce. "That was great for a while, but soon I got bored. There's only so much traveling a person can do." She eats the bite.

"What came then?"

"Then, I became someone new. It happened by accident. I was in India and met this group of college kids. Before I knew it, I was introducing myself as someone I wasn't. I put on a fake British accent and was a poor kid from London. Then I was a wilderness guide from Colorado. After that, I became one of nine kids from a sheep farmer in New Zealand. You name it and I pretended to be it as I hopped countries. I've been a teacher, an organic farmer, an esthetician." She looks at me. "I was even a veterinarian in Africa. That is until someone needed me to do surgery on a dog and I freaked."

I chuckle. "How long did you do this?"

"Long time. Up until I met Quinn."

"And when was that?"

"Four years ago now, almost one year to the date of your

leaving him." She served a mixed salad with our lasagna and while she stabs a piece of cucumber with her fork, I sip more wine. "I was in Costa Rica. He was also there, surfing. I met him on the beach. I was in between identities. He was so...emotional. I wasn't used to that in a man. Almost instantly your name came up. I became enthralled. I mean, how could a man love a woman so deeply? I couldn't get enough of him talking about you. I wanted every detail. I asked questions." She tucks an olive into her mouth. "That night I went back to my hotel and looked you up on Facebook. Your profile was private. That was easy enough to get around. I simply created a fake account, friended a bunch of your friends—by default that's public—and then you accepted my request. I even messaged you and told you we met at a medical conference. Unfortunately, you didn't remember me, but you were happy to have a new contact." She laughs. "Anyway, after that, I took detailed notes. I decided then that you would be my new identity. Plus, I'd never been a nurse before."

My fingers tighten around the stem of the wine glass.

"I was fascinated with Quinn's obsession with you. I went looking for him the next day. He taught me how to surf. We clicked. We flirted. Soon it was me he became mesmerized with, not you. He thought it was fate that he met another nurse who was raised by a single ex-military father. Then at dinner, I ordered a vegan meal and talked about hiking." She chuckles. "He was hooked. We spent a wonderful week together. I followed him back to Florida. I encouraged him to talk about you. The more I found out, the more rounded my new identity became. He was my world. But you were his. He would not let you go. Not even when I got pregnant."

I choke. "You got pregnant?"

"A little girl. He wanted to name her Jessica. That's officially when I began to hate both you and him. I ended up miscarrying during the second trimester."

I have no response. I was not expecting this.

Her emotions get the best of her. Tears wet her eyes. She takes a minute to sniff them back. "We had just had a big argument about you. It wasn't enough that I encouraged and allowed him to talk about you. I realized he was keeping track of you. The funny thing is, if you would have snapped your fingers, he would have dropped me for you in a heartbeat. You don't realize the devotion you had in him. Makes me sick how you didn't appreciate him."

I'm no longer interested in the lasagna. I put my metal fork on the ceramic plate and place it beside me on the bed.

"That's about the time he began fantasizing how he would break in and take you hostage. I encouraged it. I wanted to know the details. I wanted to make it happen." She pushes her tray table away. "Sure, I knew everything about you. But what was the big f'ing deal? That's when I decided to put his fantasies into motion." She holds her arms out. "And here I am, having dinner with the infamous Jessica."

"I'm just a normal woman. There's nothing special about me."

She huffs another laugh. "No, you are pretty damn great. I see now why he was obsessed with you. You're honest. You would have never traveled the world, blew through money, and lied to everyone about who you are."

True, I would have never done that. I'm more of the Peace Corp type.

Standing, she nods to my half-eaten dinner. "You done?"

"I am." I place my wine glass on the tray next to the dinner dishes.

Martha comes up beside the bed. Leaning over, she takes the tray. It's the closest she's been to me since putting me in here.

The half-done shiv down inside my bra pokes me. I'm almost ready to take her on.

29

Thursday 6 a.m.

ONE WEEK ago today I came over here for Chinese food and wine. I thought I had made a new friend when in fact I had stepped into a nightmare.

In the bathroom, I secretly exercise my leg. It's only been four days since I was shot, but I'm getting better and stronger each minute, each hour. I don't have time to completely heal, though. As soon as the shiv is ready, I'll make my move.

Out in the main room, the door opens. I brace myself. Tucking the weapon back down in my bra, I flush the toilet and come to stand at the bathroom entrance.

Martha hovers with just her face in a sliver of the open door, like Jack Nicholson in *The Shining*. She flashes a manic grin that twinkles through her eyes. "I have a surprise for you. But you have to leave your room."

"Okay..." I put extra emphasis on a limp as I cross over.

The door opens wide, Martha steps back, and I slide through. Popeye stands over near the steps, looking curiously around the basement.

I gasp. "Popeye!"

His head whips up. He does a whole-body wiggle, then he launches into a Flintstone-style run. His paws slide under him trying to gain traction. His little body lunges forward.

Laughing, I come down to the concrete floor, letting him collide into me.

He whines and nibbles my neck and face. I hug him tighter than I've ever hugged him. He smells so good—like fresh laundry, wet dog, and bologna. Not a great way to describe it, but somehow it works.

"Oh, I missed you." I kiss every part of his face. I rub his ears. He runs a lap around the room. I follow him the best I can. We end up back near the steps. I lie down and let him climb on top of me. He stands on my chest and licks my chin.

I don't know how much time goes by, but I finally look at Martha who's standing up at the reinforced steel door, looking down on us. I'm surprised to see happy tears glinting in her eyes.

"Thank you," I say. "Thank you so much."

She nods. "I'll let him stay. I also brought you donuts. She points to the desk where the padded chair holds a small white box.

"I appreciate this." Happy tears spring free. "Thank you."

She turns to the keypad, punches the code, and leaves.

I'm so shocked, I don't move.

Did she forget to lock me in my room?

More importantly, did she mean for me to see the new code?

30

Thursday 12 p.m.

POPEYE and I play for nearly an hour until he finally gives up. I eat one apple fritter, sharing some with him. We curl up together on the beanbag. To my knowledge, there is no camera in this part of the basement, but I still stay on my best behavior.

As I stroke his ears, I look over to the shelves, noting the toolbox is now gone. So is the first aid kit. Only books and pantry-style items remain.

On the large monitor, only one camera is displayed. It's the one covering the front porch. She's changed the angle so it no longer looks out over the Airbnb.

Her car sits in the driveway.

Eventually, I doze off. Popeye and I sleep cuddling on the beanbag.

A beep filters through the air, followed by the basement door opening. It wakes me up.

Slowly, robotically, Martha descends the steps. At the bottom, she stops. Something's different about her. From her slumped shoulders to her fallen face, she looks emotionally drained.

"You okay?" I ask.

"I don't know." She shrugs, no life to her eyes at all. "I'm just a bit depressed, I think. I mean, what am I doing? Why did I lock you up down here?"

With a sigh, she walks over to the desk. She opens the donut box, then closes it back. I note the gun once again wedged into the back of her waistband. My heart sinks. Whatever trust I earned has been lost.

"Why do I make the decisions that I make?" She picks the gun up. "I want to be a good person. I just don't know how. I can't believe I kept you from Popeye. Look how happy he makes you." She waves the gun between us. "I want to make you that happy. Does that sound weird?"

Blankly, I stare at her. "No, that sounds normal. I like pleasing people. I like helping and making their world different. It's why I became a nurse."

"But it's effortless for you. For me, it takes plotting and planning. It doesn't come naturally." She half turns, looking away from me over to the screen that still shows the front porch. "I'm thinking of letting you go."

Hope surges through me. I sit up.

Out of the corner of her eyes, she sees my movement and turns to look at me. "Well, anyway, I'm heading into town. I'll be gone most of the afternoon. Do you need anything?"

I shake my head, trying not to look at the gun.

"I'm going to lock you back up." She gestures to the door

that leads into my room. "Take the donuts you didn't eat with you."

With the gun half-heartedly aimed, she backs away, giving me room.

On my "gimp" leg, it takes me a minute to get out of the beanbag, but I do. Popeye follows me.

"No. He stays with me," she says.

Unexpected tears push at my eyes. I pick the white box up and walk it into my room. Popeye trails behind. After I place the uneaten donuts on my bed, I turn to look at him. "You be a good boy for Martha." I kiss him. "I'll see you soon." He whines as I push him out into the main area. One more kiss and I shut the door.

Popeye barks.

Tears fall.

I hate her so much.

In the bathroom, I put weight on my left leg, coming up on my toes and back down, repeating several times. I do a few two-legged squats followed by one-legged. I tighten my thighs and release them. I stretch my hamstrings, my quads, and my inner legs.

I feel good. Not perfect, but better.

Out in the bedroom, I eat another donut and I stare at the clock on the TV. She said she was leaving. I'll give her thirty minutes, then I'll retrieve the lock pick materials and get the hell out of here.

31

Thursday 12:30 p.m.

I ALLOW thirty minutes to go by before I pick the lock on my door and step out into the other side of the basement. Though Popeye isn't there, I still look over to the beanbag.

Next, my gaze goes to the security monitor. The view is the same—showing the front porch and driveway. This time, Martha's car is gone.

As quickly as I can without reinjuring my thigh, I take the steps up. At the top, I punch in the new code. The door opens.

My heart pushes pace.

I step out into the kitchen. "Popeye!"

Silence greets me.

"Popeye!"

Nothing.

I make my way into the living room, finding his dog bed empty.

She took him with her.

Does she normally take my dog when she runs errands? I don't know, but either way, I don't like it.

The windows in here look out over the large magnolias with the Airbnb beyond. Not surprisingly, no one is there.

I come from the living room, moving down the hall toward the front door. My hand reaches for the knob right as my eyes lift and I note an alarm system, engaged and ready.

Shit.

If I had my dog, I would open that door and just leave. Who cares? But if I do, Martha will take off and I'll never see Popeye again.

An archway to the left leads through the eating area. I circle the room, checking out the windows. They're all locked and wired with the alarm.

Back in the kitchen, those windows also have triggers as does the back door. The elderly deaf man who lives next door sits on his back porch, rocking in a chair and reading a book. He can't hear me, but still, I scream, "Help!" I bang the window with my fist.

The man doesn't stir.

Down the hall and up the stairs I go. Step number five squeaks as I pass over it. Surprisingly my breathing comes labored when I move into the master suite. When I first saw my Pinterest board come to life, I loved it. Now, I hate it.

"Popeye?"

Nothing.

Like downstairs, these windows are also locked and wired.

I look down to the spot on the floor where I bludgeoned my ex-husband to near death. It nauseates me. To the left, a bank of windows looks out over the front of the house, showing the nationally protected land across from our street. According to Martha, Quinn's buried somewhere out there.

Gizmo, the hamster, happily plays in a cage situated near the bay window that gives a side yard view. Crossing over, I look out, seeing my home from up here. It looks just like it did when I left a week ago, but my car is gone. I'm sure Martha moved it somewhere.

Over on the canopy bed, a pink striped scrapbook draws my attention. It's the same one I saw on the shelves in the basement.

That's private.

Martha did not want me to see this.

I look at the cover. MY LIFE. Yep, it's the same one.

The first page has a newspaper article dated almost twenty years ago. "Jackson and Kathleen Goodard die in a freak accident. They leave behind their daughter, Martha, who is set to inherit their multi-million-dollar fortune."

I flip to the next newspaper article, reading, "London girl dies in India in a freak accident."

And the next one, "Colorado wilderness guide dies in a freak accident."

The next one, "New Zealand sheep farmer dies in a freak accident."

Then, "Veterinarian dies in a freak accident while working in Africa."

"I was in India and met this group of college kids. Before I knew it, I was introducing myself as someone I wasn't. I put on a fake British accent and was a poor kid from London. Then I was a wilderness guide from Colorado. After that, I became one of

nine kids from a sheep farmer in New Zealand. You name it and I pretended to be it as I hopped countries. I've been a teacher, an organic farmer, an esthetician." She looks at me. *"I was even a veterinarian in Africa."*

Freak accident. Freak accident. Freak accident...
Another article has multiple sketches of the same woman, but with different hairstyles—wavy brown, curly red, pixy blonde, and various others. Though the sketches vary over the years, it's Martha. This one's dated four years ago, which is when she met Quinn. The headline reads, "Woman wanted in string of freak accident deaths."

I read:

Though her first name is Martha, she has many last names and many looks. She lives off of cash. But a connection was recently discovered when questioning family and friends that leads us to believe this woman could be connected to many more "freak accident" deaths.

Elizabeth, a local teacher, died in a freak accident where she accidentally inhaled too much chalk dust. According to family and friends, she had recently befriended a woman named Martha Lang, another teacher, who has since disappeared.

Kelly, an organic farmer, died in a freak accident where she fell into a tomato patch and had an allergic reaction. According to family and friends, she had recently befriended a woman named Martha Franklin, another organic farmer, who has since disappeared.

Naomi, an esthetician, died in a freak accident where she locked herself in a cryo-chamber. According to family and friends, she had recently befriended a woman named Martha Abbot, another esthetician, who has since disappeared.

Bewildered, I keep reading the article. I imagine mine:

Jessica, a nurse, died in a freak accident where she accidentally stabbed herself with a shiv. According to family and friends, she had recently befriended Martha, also a nurse, who has since disappeared with Jessica's dog, Popeye.

Including her parents, that's eight total "freak accident" deaths in nearly two decades, the first when she was just seventeen.

I may, or may not, be the first woman she's locked in a room, but I'm not her first target. Somehow that makes me feel equal parts relieved and terrified. Relieved because I'm not singled out, terrified because she knows what she's doing.

This is her thing. She moves around, befriending other women and becoming their "twin." Then when things don't go as planned (aka, they realize she's a stalker), she somehow orchestrates their "freak accident" deaths. According to the timeline, this ended four years ago, though, when she met Quinn.

What, did she think she was turning over a new leaf with my ex?

The two of them deserved each other.

After I make sure the scrapbook is exactly how I found it, I go in search of a cell phone. I doubt I'll find one, but I look anyway. I'm downstairs in the kitchen opening and closing drawers when a car pulls up outside.

Snagging a knife from the counter block, I charge down the hall. Pain twinges my thigh. I wince as I tuck in behind the front door.

I ready myself.

The engine turns off.

Then, nothing.

I don't hear her getting out of the car or walking up to the front door.

Curious, I shift a little, peering out a side window. She's sitting slumped over the wheel. A few seconds go by, then minutes. Finally, her door opens. She doesn't even glance at the house as she rounds to the trunk, and opening it, she takes out two reusable grocery bags. She closes the trunk, beeps the car lock, then walks toward the house.

Wait a minute, where's Popeye?

My fingers tighten around the knife's handle. I look down at the shiny and large, dangerous blade. I can't do this. If I attack her when she comes into the house, I risk not knowing where my dog is.

My sock-covered feet slip on the hardwood floor as I track back to the kitchen. I slide the knife into the block. A cramp sieges my thigh. Gritting my teeth, I fight it as I hurry back through the basement door. With it closed and locked, I tread the wood steps down. My gaze lifts to the monitor.

She walks through the front door.

I keep watching her car, hoping Popeye leaps into view, but he never does.

Sickness burrows into my gut. I don't know what she did with my dog, but he better be alive and at a dog spa. Because she will regret her entire existence if she harmed my Popeye.

32

Thursday 6 p.m.

SITTING IN THE BATHROOM, I continue sharpening the plastic box cutter. With each swipe across the brick wall, I say his name.

Popeye.

Popeye.

Popeye.

What did she do with him? Is that why she let me see him? Was it some sort of cruel goodbye that I didn't even know I was giving?

With my finger, I test the tip of my shiv. A sneer creeps into my lips. It's ready. I don't even need the dinky blade that came with it. This thing will do the damage needed.

Carefully, I climb to my feet. I put all my weight on my bad leg, irritated at the discomfort. I was doing so well until I went upstairs.

It doesn't matter. I'm still going to make my move on her tonight. Now. Because it's six, and she'll be here any second with my dinner. Down inside my bra, I stash the weapon. I wrap the delicate blade in toilet paper and place it in my bra too. I'm ready.

The door beeps.

Here we go.

Suddenly, the lights go out.

What the…?

I step from the bathroom out into the main area.

Martha stands in the open door, holding a flashlight directed at me.

"Did we lose power?" Squinting, I hold a hand up to cut the glare.

"Do you like it here?" she asks. "Do you have everything you need?"

"I'd love Popeye to be down here with me. I was hoping you'd bring him back."

Slowly, she reaches into the deep pocket of her denim overalls—yet something else she got from my closet.

She pulls out the gun and puts it to her head. "What would happen if I used this on myself? Would you be sad?"

Stunned, I don't speak.

"Would you?"

I nod, once.

"We both know that isn't true." She points it at me.

"Martha, what's going on?" Lowering my hand, I look right into the flashlight beam.

She fires the gun.

33

Friday 6 a.m.

VOICES COME FROM FAR AWAY. They morph in and out of my skull, some lingering, others ricocheting around. My eyes squeeze tight as I concentrate on the tone and words.

> *"...From where I was standing I could see directly into the eye of the great fish."*
> *"Mammal."*
> *"Whatever."*
> *"Well, what did you do next?"*
> *"Then from out of nowhere a huge title wave lifted, tossed like a cork..."*

With a groan, I open my eyes. One single white light pierces my skull. I groan.

Laughter tickles over me, coming from my right. "I love this episode."

I stir, trying to come to, but unable to clear the cobwebs. She drugged me again.

Seinfeld's on the TV. Martha's sitting in a chair near the door. I shift, and something rattles. My bed is missing. Instead, I'm on the floor, my ankles shackled together like the prisoner that I am. The chain connects to an eye bolt secured to the concrete.

My words come strung together in a slur. "What's going on?"

Putting the TV on mute, Martha looks at me with bright and alert eyes. Happy eyes. "I tranquilized you again with ketamine. I used enough for someone twice your size. I wanted you out for a while. I kept checking your pulse. I'm such a nurse."

"What day is it?"

"Friday, 6 a.m. You've been out all night." She holds up a gun, different than the one she shot me in the thigh with. "I'm getting to be a good shot."

"Is that a tranquilizer gun?"

"Yep, got it at Wal-Mart. It's why I went into town." Her head tilts, and her voice softens. "Did you not think I'd know?"

"Know what?"

"I can watch you via an app."

It takes my brain a moment to catch up. When I went out, the monitor on the other side of the basement showed a view of the porch and the driveway. She said the cameras were live feed only. Of course, she has an app. Just because that monitor showed one camera only doesn't mean she can't view the others.

Stupid.

I am certifiably stupid.

"The first time I overlooked your little escape. You needed those things from the first aid kit. I knew you were desperate."

I am so screwed, but I look up at her with all honesty. "I did, yes."

"Then I decided to put you through a little test. I wanted to give you the benefit of the doubt. I allowed you to see the code out of here. I left to run errands. Unfortunately, you disappointed me." Tilting her head, she looks at me. "So, I guess now you know my little secret. I saw you looking through my scrapbook."

I try to sit up, but my head spins. "Why, Martha?"

"Why, what? Try to have a friend? Try to be loyal? Try to be loved?"

Oh. My. God.

"I've never actually killed anyone. They really do have freak accidents."

"That you facilitate," I mumble.

"Mm." She shrugs. "Except for Quinn. But that was more of me putting him down, like an injured animal."

"Where's Popeye?"

"Is that why you didn't leave?" She smirks. "I knew it."

"Where is he?"

She waves her hand around my sparse cell. "The thing is, I've never done this hold-someone-captive-thing before. If it wasn't for Quinn suggesting it, I honestly would've never thought of it. And as I've been sitting here, it came to me so clearly, what I did wrong. I gave you so much from the start. I should have held everything back, allowing you to earn your privileges. Therefore, we are going to begin again. You have no bed. Nothing to snack on. No books. No personal hygiene items. Though I did leave you one washcloth that you can reuse for toilet paper. You'll find that chain you're attached to will get you to the toilet, but that's it. If you get bored, you can walk in circles. I'll also make you one meal per day. Oh, and—"

Holding up my lock-picking items, she clicks her tongue. "Boy, you're a smart thing," she says, sounding truly impressed. "You'll have to show me this clever trick at a later date."

"Where's my dog?"

"While you were knocked out, I was also thinking about how removed you are down here. Perhaps that's why you're so discontent. So, I have decided to let you keep the TV. Channel three is, of course, *Seinfeld*. Channel two now gives you multiple views of the house. You can watch me cook, sleep, read, workout..."

"Where is my dog?"

"What, no thank you? I thought the TV was very generous of me."

"Where. Is. My. Dog?"

"Now, don't get snippy." She shows me the necklace, now with two keys—one for my shackles and one for the door. "Keeping them close to my heart."

My eyes narrow.

She sighs. "It is too bad you got nosy. See I had Popeye with me, fully intending on bringing him back *if* you behaved yourself. But, again, you disappointed me. You lost privileges to him as well. I gave him to the pound. They'll find a good home for him. If not, they'll euthanize."

I shriek.

"Good day, Jessica." She leaves my room, closing and locking the door.

34

Friday 12 p.m.

I'M NOT SURE HOW, but the shiv still sits securely in my bra.

Another test? Another weird game?

I don't think so.

I didn't think there was a camera on the other side of the basement, but there is. Because I'm currently staring at the TV with its multiple views. The camera over on the other side is hidden in the keypad at the top of the steps, giving a wide-angle shot to include the shelves.

The day I first used my lock picks and went over there to explore, my back was to that camera as I teetered on the step stool, searching the shelves. She saw me dig through the first aid kit, selecting what I needed. She saw me struggle with the toolbox, but she never saw me stash the small box cutter down inside my tee shirt.

She doesn't know I have it.

On the TV Martha's upstairs in the master bedroom, snuggled on the window seat, reading to Gizmo. Propped beside her is an iPad that she periodically glances at—I'm sure looking at me.

Whatever, I don't care.

Back down here, I analyze the eye bolt, the chain, and the ankle shackles. I yank on them. Hell, if I had the pen clip and journal wire, I'd try picking the goddamn thing. I don't care if Martha sees.

Eventually, I climb to my feet. The ketamine whooshes through me, and I take a second to steady myself. The chain rattles as I limp into the bathroom, turn on the faucet, and gulp several handfuls of tepid water.

Fatigue slumps through my muscles. This time yesterday held such promise. I truly thought I'd grab Popeye and run.

I'm done playing her games.

I am going to kill this bitch.

And then I'm going to go get my dog.

35

Friday 6 p.m.

When the door opens, Martha is already talking, "When Quinn first verbalized his fantasy about holding you prisoner, I was automatically intrigued. I wasn't reluctant at all. I jumped on board so quickly that it threw him off. 'I'm just talking,' he said. 'I'm not serious.'" She snorts. "Whatever, he was totally serious. It's too bad he's not here. He would've loved this."

I flip her off.

"Oh, now, is that the way you want to treat someone who has brought you dinner?" She steps forward, placing a paper bowl with oatmeal just within my reach. "Breakfast for dinner."

I lunge for her, and the chain snaps me back.

Grabbing the paper bowl, I hurl it at her. Quickly, she

sidesteps. The oatmeal splatters and clumps across the floor in an unsatisfying mess.

Laughing, she takes the keys from around her neck. She swings the necklace back and forth, surveying the mess. "I'm sure not cleaning that up. If you get hungry, you know where your meal is."

I scream.

The door closes.

36

Saturday 6 a.m.

I sit on the floor with my back to the wall.

The door opens. Martha looks at the oatmeal mess I've yet to clean up. She clicks her tongue, scolding me.

Despite the fact I'm the one chained, I feel strong and in control.

Holding up a paper plate with a bagel sandwich on it, she says, "I have to say, you've once again disappointed me. You should have cleaned that oatmeal up. Guilt was gnawing at me. I was going to treat you to a breakfast sandwich, but now I'm not."

My jaw grits tight.

A few beats go by.

"Tell you what, you did such a great job rewriting your and Quinn's history. Write more. Write that love scene I mentioned. But make it me and Quinn, not you and Quinn.

Ooh, make it our wedding night. I'll go get the silver journal and a fresh pen." Her eyes narrow. "One without a clip." She straightens. "Yes, write that and I'll clean up your spilled oatmeal and make you whatever meal you would like."

"No deal."

"Hm." She takes a bite of the bagel sandwich. "Wow, this is good. Egg, cheese, and sausage. Too bad you're vegan. Though if you get hungry enough, you'll eat meat I'm sure."

"Get out."

"Or you can talk me through the wedding night. You don't have to write it. I'm not hard to work with. I can negotiate."

"GET OUT."

Martha holds up a hand. "Fine, geez," she says, her tone full of snark. "You don't have to be so irritable."

I think she's going to leave, but she doesn't. She stands there, eating the breakfast sandwich, staring at me.

"WHAT?" I explode.

"Just trying to figure you out."

"What's to figure out? You locked me in this room. You shot me in the thigh. You've tranquilized me twice. You've taunted me. Tortured me. Got rid of my dog. You have me chained to the floor." I stand up. "What else are you going to do? If you've got some 'freak accident' in mind for me, you might as well get to it. I'm right here. Give it your best shot."

"I am good to you." Another bite. She swallows. "Look at what you used to have. A bed, a crate of snacks, a bathroom, home-cooked meals, I even did your laundry when you soiled yourself. You've brought this on yourself. You need to focus on being a better friend."

No, I need to focus on stabbing you with this shiv.

37

Sunday 12 p.m.

THE REST of the day goes by. So does the next morning. I don't see Martha. Unfortunately, my hunger wins out and I eat the dried and clumpy oatmeal off the floor.

I'm standing watching her on the TV make cookies when someone walks up her driveway.

Dragging the chain along with me, I move closer to the screen, leaning in to see.

My eyes widen. My hand comes out, spreading wide on his image.

Dad.

Tears fill my eyes.

For a moment, he stands, looking to the left where my house sits two over. Then he studies Martha's home.

Fixated at the sight of him, my heart races. I both want

him to ring her bell and also not. What if she does something to him?

Slowly, he walks across her yard and up the porch steps. He knocks on the door.

In the kitchen, Martha looks up. Wiping her hands on a towel, she glances at the iPad sitting on the island countertop. She studies the small screen, frowning a bit. I'm not sure if she knows what my father looks like.

She leaves the kitchen, trailing the hall to the front door.

I track her movements as she flows across the multiple views I have.

She opens the door.

My finger shakes as I press the volume up button on the TV.

Dad's voice soothes and coats my soul. "Hello, my name is Reece Prather. I'm Jessica Prather's father. She lives two doors down from you. Do you know her?"

"I do, yes." A sweet smile curves Martha's face.

"Have you seen her?"

"Um, yes, about a week ago. Thursday night. She helped me unpack. I'm new to the neighborhood. We had Chinese food together. I met her dog, Popeye." Her head tilts, all charm and innocence. "Why, is everything okay?"

"I'm not sure."

"Do you live around here?" Martha asks.

"No, I live in Florida. Drove all night to get here."

She brightens. "Oh, I love Florida!"

An odd smile crosses his face. "Well, if you see her, will you let her know I'm looking for her?"

"Have you tried her work?"

"They're the ones who called me. Someone reported that we were in an accident together. They were checking to see if we were doing better."

"Oh...that's odd."

"Yes, it is odd."

Martha's cheeks flare in embarrassment. "Would you like to come in?" She steps aside. "I'm about to take cookies from the oven. I also have something that belongs to Jessica. She left it here the night she came over to help me unpack."

No. My head shakes. *No, Dad, don't come in.*

"Sure, I guess. Thanks." He steps through the door.

Martha closes it, glancing up at the hallway camera with a smirk.

I slap the TV and scream.

Idly, Dad checks things out as he follows Martha down the hall and into the kitchen.

Over her shoulder, she smiles at him. "My father's ex-military, just like you. Plus, I'm a nurse. Crazy coincidence, huh?"

His brow twitches. "Yeah, that is a coincidence."

In the kitchen, she turns off the oven and opens the door to pull out the cookies.

Dad wanders around the small area, checking out the windows and back door wired with the alarm, the basement with the keypad, and the camera mounted above the refrigerator.

"I've got a deranged ex-husband," Martha says, noticing Dad's eye movement. "Jessica mentioned she also had a looney one. Another weird coincidence, huh?"

At the kitchen island, Dad stops. He focuses down on the wood floor. I can't tell what he's looking at.

"I wondered why I hadn't seen her since that night." Martha slides the cookies onto a cooling rack. "I thought maybe I'd offended her or something."

"Why do you have Popeye's bowl?" Dad points to where he's looking.

"That's why I invited you in. She left that here."

Our conversations are few and far between, but my father knows Popeye is my world. I can't see the bowl from this angle, but I'm sure it's the custom one I had made with his name engraved. I told my dad about that bowl during one of our rare conversations.

Red flags are going off. It's all over his face. He knows I would never leave that bowl here.

"Gosh, I like your daughter. She's very sweet." Martha places a cookie on a paper towel and hands it to my father. "You have no idea where she is?"

"No, I don't."

Sadly, she shakes her head.

Leaning down, Dad picks up the bowl. He pours what water is left in it down the sink.

"Do you want a tour of the house?" She laughs. "Sorry if that's weird. I'm a first-time homeowner. I'm excited. The other day I asked the UPS man if he wanted one."

"No, thank you. I need to get going." Dad takes the cookie from her.

"Oh, sure. Would you like my number? Ya know, in case you need anything?"

"That's okay. I know where you live." He leaves the kitchen. During the trek back to the front door, he notes the hallway camera as well, looking directly into it. His brows come down.

"Dad," I whisper.

Martha lingers in the kitchen. From the knife block on the island, she selects the largest one. It's the same one I had in my hand just days ago. Her sneaky leer cuts up to the camera mounted above the refrigerator. She taunts me—rotating the knife in the air. Then with it held behind her back, she saunters from the room.

Down the hall, my father reaches the front door. My pulse elevates. Please, just go. Walk out the door, Dad. NOW.

Martha appears behind him. "You going to be in the area long?"

"As long it takes, I suppose." He opens the door.

"You'll be staying at Jessica's place?" She shifts, bringing the knife further up on her back.

"Yes." He steps onto the porch, turning to look at her. "Thank you for the cookie and the bowl."

"You're welcome. See you around." She stands on the porch in plain view of the camera, watching him walk back over to my house.

On the sidewalk, he pauses, looking back at her.

She smiles, watching him.

He keeps walking, eventually disappearing.

She looks up at the porch camera. "Did you think I would stab your father?" Her eyes brim with enthusiasm. "Oh, you."

38

Sunday 6 p.m.

THE DOOR OPENS. Quietly, Martha enters. She notes the oatmeal eaten off the concrete. This enthralls her. "I knew you'd get hungry." She places a paper plate with cookies on the floor and slides it across to me. One tumbles off. "I liked your dad. It's too bad it takes something like this to get him to appear."

I grab a cookie and devour it. It's cranberry-white chocolate, my favorite. I eat it so fast, hating how good it tastes.

With eyes on me, she inches into the room to take the paper bowl the oatmeal was in.

I am more than ready to attack this woman, but she won't get close enough for me to do so. She knows exactly how far my chain will allow movement. I have to figure out how to lure her in.

On the floor, I shift from one hip to the other. Martha

leaps back. She's scared. That's good. Inside my bra, something pokes me, but it's not the shiv. It's the tiny blade. I wince.

"Your leg hurt?"

"Yes," I lie.

"Do you need Tylenol? I also have Advil."

"No, I like the pain."

She hesitates.

I throw my arms out to the side, taunting. "Go on, Martha. Kill me. I'm done. I don't care."

She stares hard, not moving. I visualize her wheels turning, weighing my words like she could go either way on this. Killing me is pretty far down on the list, though. She likes this game of keeping me locked up and outsmarting the world.

I have to figure out how to lure her in.

An idea sneaks in.

It curls through me—effective, but scary.

I know exactly how to get her closer…

39

Monday 6 a.m.

THE REST of the night I sit curled against the wall, concentrating on the three remaining cookies still on the paper plate. Madness crawls through me. I doubt my decision. What if I die? I might. The chance is great. It's a gamble, the thing I plan to do, but Martha has left me no choice.

I glance up to the corner where the hidden camera is mounted in a globe light. I don't know if she's watching, but my gut says yes.

Turning my back on her view, I reach down inside my bra, taking out the two weapons. I tuck the shiv into the waistband of my leggings, covering it with my tee shirt. My fingers tremble as I unwrap the toilet paper from the thin blade.

I position it on my left wrist. A shallow horizontal cut will bring lots of blood but not death. Vertical brings death.

This won't be clean like a scalpel. It will be jagged and messy. Those two words alone pitch nausea straight to my throat.

Okay, Jessica, you can do this.

My teeth clench as I muster the courage. Pressing down into the thin skin, I drag it horizontally across my left wrist. Despite my best efforts, I cry out. The nearly transparent skin peels away. My veins pulse. Blood oozes. I swallow the bile that bitters my mouth.

I do my right wrist.

Then I fold the thin blade into my sock and I turn, giving the camera a full shot of my slit wrists.

"I hate you!" I scream.

A moment goes by. The room tilts. I lie down on the floor, my arms flayed with my wrists up. More blood seeps out. My eyes close.

Another moment goes by. More blood pulses. Clamminess creeps along my skin. Behind my closed eyes, the darkness swirls.

One more minute beats by. White dots appear, dancing and floating through the swirling darkness. Oddly, I smell Popeye. I hear his high-pitched happy whine.

I pray I find him alive.

Another minute creeps by. My body sags fully into the concrete floor. I doubt my decision to do this.

The door opens. Martha bursts in. I don't move. Her feet slide across the floor as she swoops down on me. "What have you done?"

She comes down next to me, picking up my right slit wrist. "Oh my God." She presses her palm to it, but that only smears the seeping blood. She hurries into the bathroom.

The Lady Next Door

My fingers shift, sliding the shiv from my waistband. With it seated firmly in my right palm, I adjust my hand to hide it.

I ready myself.

She hurries back, coming down, as I had hoped, on the side closest to the bathroom—my left side. With shaking hands, she presses the washcloth to my left wrist. "Jessica, can you hear me?"

All my rage binds together into a tight ball. It wells inside of me. With a scream, I explode up. My right-hand punches out and I seat the shiv into her neck. Blood bursts from the hole.

For a brief few seconds, Martha stares into my eyes, transfixed. Then all hell reigns down. She shakes off her surprise and fights back, grabbing me with both hands. She tries to shove me away, but my fingers stay tightly gripped on the sharpened box cutter. I yank it out and with all my power, I plunge it back in. This time I get her in the shoulder. From her scream, I hope I tore through a muscle.

I drive her to the floor and climb on top. I don't let go of the weapon as I rip it out. I'm just about to plunge it back in when she shoves me. Hard. I go flying. So does my weapon.

Martha struggles to her feet. She produces the gun, though which one I don't know—the tranquilizer or the one with real bullets. She fumbles to shoot it but I quickly sweep my chained feet, knocking her back down to her ass.

With a yell, I tackle her. We go down hard. The gun careens and spins across the concrete floor. I wrestle my knees into her arms, holding her down. Wildly, she bucks underneath me.

I punch her in the mouth. "Die you goddamn lunatic. DIE."

My fist collides with her nose. Her head slams to the floor. I don't care. I hit her again.

Martha's face quickly swells. She spits and screams, shrieks and jerks. But I keep my knees firmly in her arms. One last hard jerk from her causes me to lose my balance. I topple over. She tries to crawl away. The chain connecting my ankles to the eye bolt rattles. I scramble after her, once again sweeping my legs, this time I snake the chain around her ankles. I yank. She falls face down into the concrete. I drag her toward me.

She screams and claws at the floor.

My fingers dig into her hips. I pull her closer as I crawl onto her back. Planting my feet on both sides of her head, I work the chain under her face to her neck. I yank, *hard*. Her body bows off the floor. She gurgles and thrashes. Her arms windmill as she twists. Blood spurts from the wound in her neck. It opens even more. The sight of it surges fresh adrenaline through me.

I wrench harder, choking...

Choking...

Choking...

One last gurgle. Her body falls limp.

Exhausted, panting, I don't move. My muscles quiver as I slowly give the chain slack. I fall from her back to the side. Broken capillaries spread through her cheeks, into her eyes. I stare at them as I remove the silver chain and keys from around her neck.

Through her mouth, Martha inhales a quick breath, followed closely by a shriek.

It startles me enough that I don't react. Her body surges up until she stands in a strong and relentless, looming pose. Her swollen nose pulses with blood. I scramble back. My hand connects with the gun. I swerve it up.

I point.

I shoot.

Time suspends. Martha's body hovers above the ground. Fresh blood darkens her shirt near the same shoulder I stabbed. She falls straight back. Her head bounces off the concrete.

With everything I have left, I come to my knees. I point the gun again. I shoot. But no bullet comes.

Martha doesn't move.

I try again with the gun. No bullet comes. I throw it to the side. Using the key, I unlock my shackles. I clamber from the room. On the steps up, I trip. But I make it to the top. My finger fumbles with the code.

The door opens. I collapse into the kitchen, scratching and clawing my way down the hall to the front door.

The first light of morning breaks through as I erupt from her house.

"Dad! Dad! Help me! Help me!" My sock-covered feet pound across Martha's yard, the Airbnb next door, and over onto my property. Dad's car sits in my driveway. "Dad! Help!" I pound on the front door. "HELP!"

It swings open.

I fall limp into his arms.

40

M *onday 7 a.m.*

I NOW SIT in the back of an ambulance with my father's arm wrapped around me. A paramedic has already wrapped my wrists and is performing a quick exam before taking me to the hospital.

Two doors down and with guns drawn, cops have already entered Martha's home.

Blood pulses and pounds through my veins. I stare hard at her front door, waiting to see the body bag brought out.

Five minutes turns to ten. Ten to twenty. But still, I stare. The paramedic wants to leave, but I say, "No, not until I see them bring her out."

Instead, a detective steps from her door. He looks over my house and me in the back of the ambulance.

His shoulders lift with a heavy breath. He walks across

her yard and down the sidewalk, coming to a stop at the ambulance. He looks first at Dad, then me.

"Where is she?" I ask, my voice edgy as hell.

"Don't know. Lots of blood. But she's gone. Went out the back door."

41

One Year Later

AFTER KISSING POPEYE GOODBYE, I walk into my garage and climb into my car. I hit the visor remote and the door cranks up. I turn on my car and as I back out, I roll my window down to let the cool spring air flow over me.

I moved to upstate New York not long after everything that happened with Martha, the lady next door. I took a work-from-home nursing-admin job where I coordinate trauma transports. I also have a new name to protect myself. I now reside as Rachel Perez.

The only person who knows my real identity is my father. He still lives in Florida and we talk or text nearly every day. It is the one positive thing to have come from my time as a prisoner.

The drive to town goes by quickly. I reference my list,

stopping first at the pet store for Popeye's vitamins, then the drugstore for face wash and lotion, then the park.

I like coming here on Monday morning. It's always empty. It's the only morning like that. Between lawn yoga, Mommy and Me classes, arts and crafts, and other various things, Monday remains the token time to be here.

Alone.

I pull into my usual spot and park. After checking the time, I feed my hair through a baseball cap and slide sunglasses on.

Through the trees, she walks briskly toward the bench where she sits every Monday, a book cradled to her chest. Her curly blond hair bounces with her hippy walk. Today she wears a pink tracksuit. Last Monday she wore blue. The Monday before that, white.

With her back to me, she sits on the bench and opens a book.

I slip from the driver's side. Softly, I tread across the grass and into the trees. Flipping a page of the book, she crosses her right leg over her left.

Silently, I step from the foliage.

A tiny wind kicks up, sending the scent of plumeria body wash into the air. It twines up my nostrils, making them delicately flare. I've never been a fan of flowery shampoos and soaps.

From the front pocket of my sweat pants, I extract the hypodermic needle loaded with ketamine. Holding it in plain sight, I move around the bench, coming to stand in front of her. She looks up. Her eyes widen.

I smile. "Hello, Martha."

EPILOGUE

Martha's right.
 It *is* hard digging a grave.

ABOUT THE AUTHOR

S. E. Green is the award-winning and best-selling author of young adult and adult fiction. She grew up in Tennessee where she dreaded all things reading and writing. She didn't even read her first book for enjoyment until she was twenty-five. After that, she was hooked! When she's not writing, she's usually traveling or hanging out with a rogue armadillo that frequents her coastal Florida backyard.

BOOKS BY S. E. GREEN

Before Then Now

Ten Years Later

The Family

Sister Sister

Silence

Unseen

The Strangler

The Suicide Killer

Monster

The Third Son

Vanquished

Mother May I

Printed in Great Britain
by Amazon